"Worried about our waltz, Miss Caxton?"

The earl gently teased Rowena as he led her onto the floor.

"No, my lord," she said with just the right touch of lightness. "Though I may be unfamiliar with the steps, I have no doubt but that you will direct me, for I am familiar with your autocratic ways."

"Touché," he said, laughing in appreciation, and soon, as Rowena had predicted, they were waltzing in perfect harmony.

"Now that I am sure you will not step on my feet, you may come a little closer." He pulled her towards him until only the few inches required by propriety separated them.

His hand holding hers, his strong arm about her waist, the warmth of his breath on her cheek, all should have flustered her. Instead, she felt as if she belonged in his arms. Guided, protected, cared for. But he must never know.

Summoning up all her determination, she smiled sweetly and said, "Any further orders, my lord?"

The earl laughed once again and swept her away, much to her relief. But though she had succeeded in fooling the earl, Rowena knew she could no longer fool herself.

D1599031

Books by Carola Dunn

HARLEQUIN REGENCY ROMANCE
25–A SUSCEPTIBLE GENTLEMAN

A POOR RELATION
CAROLA DUNN

Harlequin Books

TORONTO • NEW YORK • LONDON
AMSTERDAM • PARIS • SYDNEY • HAMBURG
STOCKHOLM • ATHENS • TOKYO • MILAN

Published December 1990

ISBN 0-373-31139-7

CHAPTER ONE

PINK CHEEKED AND BREATHLESS after the gallop, Rowena Caxton slipped down from the back of her sorrel mare with the aid of her groom's steadying hand. She was close enough to the house to hear a clock chime eleven somewhere inside.

"Oh, dear, I am late!" she exclaimed, picking up the train of her grey cloth riding habit. "Thank you, Tom. I doubt I shall ride again today."

"Right, miss." He grinned in response to her smile and led the mare and his own cob away as she hurried through the back door of Chillenden Manor.

Budgen popped out of the butler's pantry to announce that the lawyer from London awaited her in the library. He followed her to the flagstoned hall, a chilly place even in June, furnished with a few dark, heavy Jacobean chairs along the whitewashed walls. She tossed her whip and gloves on the matching table, took off her hat and was making a futile effort to tidy her hair when Miss Pinkerton scurried in, looking flustered, as usual.

"There you are at last, Rowena. Mr. Harwin arrived some minutes ago. The Dover mail was early, for a wonder. My dear, your hair!"

In her muddled way, she patted her own silver-grey locks under their becoming lacy cap as if that would help untangle the cascade of light brown curls tumbling down Rowena's back.

"I did tie it back, Pinkie," Rowena assured her elderly cousin, a twinkle in her green eyes. "A low branch in the orchards snagged the ribbon. Tell me, pray, ought I to keep Mr. Harwin waiting while I change and make myself respectable?"

Her composure restored by this appeal to her knowledge of etiquette, Miss Pinkerton considered the question with care.

"I believe you had best go in at once," she decided. "Gentlemen are always so impatient, your poor father excepted of course, and I daresay a lawyer will not be concerned with your appearance. Shall I come with you? Or no, I shall wait next door in the parlour with the door open and you must call if you need me."

"I doubt Mr. Harwin has any designs on my virtue. He is a most respectable gentleman and quite middle-aged."

"Really, Rowena, you must not say such... I only meant that if you have need of my support... Lawyers do tend to be birds of ill omen, you know, and they will wear those horridly depressing black coats."

"In my experience, lawyers are less likely to bring ill news than sheaves of papers to be signed. Only recollect the stack he produced when Papa died! There, that is the best I can do with my wretched hair. I shall go in, Budgen."

The lawyer rose and bowed as the butler announced Rowena. He was indeed clad all in black, but his round, kindly face with its gold rimmed spectacles did not appear in the least ominous, in spite of his worried air.

"Pray forgive my unpunctuality, Mr. Harwin," she said gaily. She sat down, the train of her habit heaped about her feet. "As you see, I did not even stop to change. I have been in the cherry orchard. We shall harvest next week, but in the meantime it has been invaded by starlings."

"Not a serious problem, I trust, Miss Caxton?"

"No, indeed. I have hired a dozen boys from the village to scare them off. They are enjoying themselves excessively, I assure you, and I daresay they will leave more of the crop than the birds would." Rowena's green eyes lit with amused resignation.

The lawyer sighed. "You have made a great success of farming Chillenden since the sad loss of your mother," he said. "It is a pity that the late Mr. Caxton took so little interest in the estate."

"No, Papa was much too caught up in his translation of Ovid's *Metamorphoses* to care about apples and greenfly and pruning. I know he would have made an effort to understand such things, though, had he not fallen ill when Mama died. He was far from well for some years, you know."

Mr. Harwin sighed again. "I fear his death has left you in a sorry situation, Miss Caxton."

"Oh, no, you must not think I am dissatisfied. I was very unhappy at first, of course. Papa was the dearest of men, though so very absentminded. But it is nine months since he died, I shall soon be out of mourning, and life goes on. To tell the truth, I am too busy to repine. I am fortunate in having dear Pinkie to run the household, but between managing the orchards, helping the tenants with their problems, and exchanging visits with the neighbours, I assure you my days are filled."

"And is there no young man among your neighbours with whom you might—ahem—seek a closer union, shall we say?"

She smiled at his circumlocution. "Marriage, you mean."

She thought of Geoffrey Farnhouse, whose father's land adjoined her own. Sir Edward Farnhouse had been an invaluable source of advice when she had found herself, at sixteen, with an invalid father and a neglected estate. She had grown up with Geoff and he was a good friend. Since well before her father's death he had been pressing her to marry him, to join the two estates. It would be a respectable match and she was fond of both him and his family, but they did not pretend to love each other.

Besides, unlike his father, he strongly disapproved of her interest in farming and was incredulous of her ability.

The lawyer was looking at her in hopeful enquiry.

"No," she said, her voice firm. "There is no one I wish to marry."

"Dear me, dear me." He took off his spectacles and polished them on a huge, red-spotted handkerchief. "It would be the ideal solution," he said wistfully.

"Solution?"

Mr. Harwin suddenly became very busy with the papers on the table beside him. "I fear I have bad news, Miss Caxton," he mumbled, avoiding her eye.

To his astonishment, she laughed. It seemed Pinkie was right. "I beg your pardon, sir," she said soberly, noting that he had taken offence. "I do not mean to make light of the matter, whatever it is."

He found the document he was looking for, glanced at it with distaste and hurriedly buried it again in the pile, shaking his head in distress.

"What is wrong, Mr. Harwin?" Rowena heard the alarm in her own voice and tried to steady it. "Pray tell me. Perhaps the problem is not as bad as you suppose."

"Worse, Miss Caxton, worse. There is a mortgage. A mortgage on..." Again he disinterred the paper, this time peering at the writing as if he hoped it might say something different by now. "...On 'Chillenden Manor, in the County of Kent, its lands, farms and all appurtenances thereto.' I fear, Miss Caxton, I greatly fear, that the mortgage has recently fallen due and the manor will have to be sold to pay it."

The room swam before Rowena's eyes. She closed them, gripping the arms of her chair in convulsive fingers.

"Chillenden! No!"

Through a fog of half-disbelieving despair, she was aware of the lawyer patting her hand, ringing the bell, calling for brandy. Budgen and Miss Pinkerton rushed in. The butler hurried to the cabinet where Rowena's father's medicinal brandy still stood, while Pinkie fanned her with a convenient copy of the *Agricultural Gazette*.

"What did you say to the poor child?" Miss Pinkerton glared at Mr. Harwin indignantly. "I've no opinion of lawyers, and so I tell you to your face."

Mr. Harwin, hovering helpless nearby, turned bright red and spluttered an incoherent protest.

Rowena pushed away the glass of amber liquid Budgen offered her. In his anxiety for her he had forgotten to put it on a tray, and she thought how she would tease him about it later, for he had far more respect for the niceties than she did. Then she realized that there would be no later.

"There must be some mistake," she said.

That was pushing Mr. Harwin too far. "No mistake," he said loudly and firmly. "Permit me to explain, Miss Caxton."

"In a moment." Rowena regained her self-control. "Thank you, Budgen. I am quite recovered. I shall call if I need you," she added as the butler showed signs of intending to stay and protect her.

The faithful servant withdrew reluctantly, with many a backward glance. "I'll be just outside the door, miss, if you need me," he announced.

"Pinkie..."

"I am here, dear, and here I shall stay. I shall not interrupt unless that man upsets you again." Miss Pinkerton perched on the chair next to Rowena's, took her hand in a comforting clasp and scowled at Mr. Harwin.

The lawyer wiped his forehead with his spotted handkerchief, polished his glasses again and sat down.

"Are you sure you are well enough for me to continue, ma'am?"

"Yes, I must understand."

"I regret to say that the document was only discovered a fortnight since. You may recollect the disarray in which the late Mr. Caxton left his papers."

"His business papers." The corners of Rowena's lips turned up in a sad, reminiscent smile. "Papa's literary papers could not have been neater."

Mr. Harwin coughed. "Yes, well," he murmured. "Be that as it may, upon his decease I removed to London an entire deskful, an accumulation of some of the

most haphazard records I have ever seen. One of my
clerks has been working on them since then. He came
upon a number of notes of hand, for considerable sums,
all marked paid. It seemed that Mr. Caxton had at various times borrowed heavily, not surprising when you
consider his lack of interest in his estate, but that he had
succeeded in redeeming the notes. However, by the time
he had found five or six, my clerk noticed that they had
all been paid on the same date. This naturally suggested a consolidated debt.''

"He mortgaged Chillenden to pay off the other
loans. Oh, poor Papa!''

POOR PAPA, SHE THOUGHT AGAIN some three weeks
later. Unable to face reality, he had pushed the prom-
issory note into the back of the desk and forgotten it,
leaving his daughter to deal with the result alone.

Rowena was riding her sorrel mare round Chillenden
for the last time. Once set in motion, events had moved
fast, and the estate was to be auctioned the day after
next. She could not bear to see her home sold. She
would be gone by then. Miss Pinkerton had already
tearfully departed to live with her brother's autocratic
widow.

There had been little choice in the planning of Rowena's future. After the battle of Toulouse in March and
Bonaparte's abdication in April, land prices were down,
and heading lower at the prospect of a poor harvest.
Mr. Harwin doubted that there would be more than a
couple of hundred pounds left to her, at most, after the
sale. Geoffrey Farnhouse, his eyes full of pity, had
proposed again. Her pride would not let her accept as
a pauper what she had refused when she thought she
had a prosperous estate for her dowry. Her education

in the classics and fruit farming had not fitted her to be a governess, the last resort of many a poverty-stricken lady of quality. And no one was likely to hire a female as a boys' tutor or a land agent.

Two courses were left open to her: to become a paid companion to a stranger, or to throw herself on the mercy of her mother's sister and go to live with her as a poor relation.

At first it seemed that the second of even these meagre alternatives was impossible. Lady Grove had made no attempt to communicate with her brother-in-law or her niece since Mrs. Caxton's death five years since. Her direction could not be found. Then Mr. Harwin's clerk recalled seeing the name Grove scribbled on the back of an old receipt, along with an address. His encyclopedic memory produced the name of the merchant on the receipt, which was duly found filed under the first letter of that name.

A grateful Mr. Harwin promptly raised his salary a shilling a week, and Rowena wrote to her aunt.

Lady Grove replied at once.

Trotting through the apple orchard, where the green fruit were beginning to swell on the branches, Rowena thought about the letter with an uneasy feeling.

Aunt Hermione had not hesitated to invite her to make her home at Grove Park. She assured her niece that Sir Henry was equally ready to receive her, and Millicent and Anne would be delighted to welcome a cousin so near to them in age. It would be quite unnecessary for Rowena to bring her mare to augment her uncle's stables, as Millicent did not ride, so there would rarely be any need for a mount.

Rowena leaned down and hugged her beloved Vixen, who snorted in surprise. She would miss riding, for she often spent half the day at Chillenden on horseback. Was that why she dreaded going into Gloucestershire? She was spoiled, used to having her own way, she thought. As a poor relation, however welcome, she must do her best to fit into the pattern of life in a strange household. She had no choice; unlike poor Papa she had to face the facts.

The next morning she dressed in a plain grey round gown and drab bonnet, suitable for travelling, and bade the servants a sad farewell. The groom drove her in the gig to Bishopsbourne to catch the Dover-to-London stage. He wanted to wait with her at the Four Feathers, to see her safely aboard the coach.

"No, Tom," she said with a tremulous smile, "I shall do very well by myself. Go home... back to Chillenden to help them prepare for the auction."

The little inn opened directly onto the village street. It seemed deserted; in fact the whole village was unusually quiet for a sunny July morning. No one answered Tom's halloo. With a sigh and a shake of the head he unloaded her trunk from the gig and set it near a bench by the inn door. Reluctantly he drove off.

Dry-eyed, Rowena watched her last link with Chillenden disappear round a bend in the road.

CHAPTER TWO

As THE HIRED POST CHAISE PASSED a slow-moving stagecoach and rattled out of Dover, Major Christopher Scott, sitting with his back to the horses, caught a last glimpse of masts in the harbour. He shuddered at the sight.

The Channel crossing had been the worst part of a dreadful journey. In the four months since the battle of Toulouse, after despairing of Bernard's life, he had watched his friend gradually recover from his wounds. The trip across France, on roads always bad and now long neglected, had set the recovery back at least a month. A rough voyage, complicated by seasickness, had completed the *débâcle* when a particularly violent bout of retching tore open the captain's shoulder injury.

It was not a propitious homecoming to the land they had fought for across Portugal and Spain and into France.

The last houses of Dover fell behind, and they left the cobbled street for the smoother highroad. Bernard, half reclining on the opposite seat, opened his eyes and grinned crookedly.

"I'm not at all certain that the ruts of France are not preferable to the cobbles of Merrie England," he said, wincing as he shifted to a more comfortable position.

"We ought to have stayed longer at the King's Head."

"And landed wholly in the basket! Your pockets are as much to let as mine, Chris, and the sooner we reach London and our bankers the better."

"Not to mention a halfway competent sawbones," said the major drily.

"It would be nice to get that piece of metal out of my shoulder," acknowledged Bernard. He closed his eyes again, his thin face very white.

Chris leaned his dark head back against the squabs. Despite his worry, he was filled with delight as he gazed out of the window. The sun shone on the rich, peaceful countryside of Kent, spreading to the horizon on either side of the road. Green orchards and golden cornfields contrasted with his memories of devastated France. Before the Peninsula War he had spent most of his life in London, but it was of fields and woods and streams he had dreamed, bivouacking in wretched huts in the arid Spanish mountains.

Bernard must see the London doctors, then he would take him down to stay with his sister and her husband in Dorset. The country air would do his friend a world of good.

The captain seemed to have fallen asleep. With luck he would not wake until they stopped to change horses in Canterbury.

The post chaise rolled smoothly through village after village. The road was busy, for since Boney's abdication, trade with the Continent was back on its old footing. They passed several wagons, and their coachman had pulled out to overtake another when he saw a sporting curricle dashing towards him. He reined in his team sharply, swinging back onto his own side of the road. The curricle bowled safely past, its fashionable driver saluting the cursing coachman with a flourish of his whip.

Inside the chaise, the unexpected manoeuvre sent Chris sliding across his seat. Cursing as fluently as the coachman, he saw Bernard, half-asleep, reach out to brace himself and moan in agony. A red patch blossomed on his shoulder and he fainted.

It was impossible even to take off his coat in such confined quarters. The major ordered the coachman to stop at the nearest inn, then he ripped off his neckcloth, folded it and thrust the pad inside his friend's shirt. Holding it, he sat beside him and tried to steady him against the jolt as they started off again.

Fortunately they were just entering a village, and moments later they pulled up in front of a small, whitewashed hostelry. The swinging sign over the door, depicting a bouquet of dyed ostrich plumes, proclaimed it to be the Four Feathers.

"Ho, landlord!" bellowed the coachman.

A slim young woman in a grey gown hurried out of the inn.

"The landlord is not here," she said. "There's no one but the cook."

"Come here, girl, and help me," called Chris impatiently, wishing he had not given his batman leave to visit his family. "I've an injured man here."

She looked surprised but obeyed. Between them they lifted Bernard down from the coach and carried him into the taproom since the place offered no better. It smelled of stale beer. They laid him on a wooden settle, and Chris was about to try to extricate him from his coat when there was an angry shout outside.

"You had best go deal with your coachman," said the young woman in a soft, low voice. "The ostlers seem to have disappeared along with the rest. You may leave your friend in my care for a moment. I shan't let him bleed to death."

Chris looked at her doubtfully. She seemed to be clean and competent, and she must be stronger than she appeared since she had helped him to carry Bernard, no light weight. Another shout decided him. He shrugged, nodded and strode out.

"I can't stay here," said the coachman indignantly. "'Tain't a proper coaching inn. First stage'll take you to Canterbury."

When Chris paid him off he grumbled that he had been hired to London. He found himself facing the icy grey gaze of Major Scott of the Second Dragoons, and he quailed. Touching his forelock, he dropped the money into his pocket and whipped up the horses.

Chris went back into the inn, hoping that the absent landlord would accept *louis d'or.* He feared their stay at the Four Feathers might be a long one and his purse was the lighter now by a couple of gold sovereigns.

The girl was kneeling beside Bernard, her hand inside his shirt. He was still unconscious. She had taken off his cravat, presumably to fashion a new pad, for a blood-soaked cloth lay on the floor nearby. She looked up as Chris entered, and he saw that she had green eyes, worried now.

"He is bleeding badly, I fear. Was it highwaymen?"

"It is a war wound." Belatedly he recognized that her accent was not that of a serving maid. "Thank you for your assistance, ma'am. I can manage now."

"I doubt it. According to the cook everyone is gone to see some hoard of Roman coins dug up by a farm hand. You will need help to take off his coat at least."

"Is there a doctor in the village?" Chris wasted no time arguing. As he spoke he gently worked Bernard's unhurt right arm out of the sleeve while she steadied his inert body on the bench.

"I think not. We always sent to Canterbury for Dr. Benson."

"Damn! The coachman went that way and I never thought to send a message."

He raised Bernard's shoulders and the young lady managed to pull the coat out from underneath. Together they eased the injured limb out of the left sleeve.

"I am going on the stage to London. It will stop in Canterbury. I shall sent the doctor to you."

Chris nodded in gratitude, too concerned to speak. Bernard's shirt was crimson all down the side, the new cloth pad already soaked through. His heart sank as he realized he had left their portmanteaux in the chaise; the rest of their luggage had been sent ahead to London.

The girl hurried towards the door, picked up a bandbox, and brought it back. Opening it, she took out a linen shift and began to tear it.

"No!" he said, "you must not."

She smiled up at him. "Have you anything else? I daresay we might find something in the inn but whether it would be fit for such a use is another matter. This is clean, I assure you."

He flushed. "I do not doubt it, ma'am. For my friend's sake I accept. I fear it is too late to be of use to you anyway." He looked ruefully at the ruined garment and smiled at her.

With one accord they turned to bind Bernard's wound.

They had nearly finished this delicate task when the landlord bustled in, full of apologies, followed by his staff. He sent the ostler at a gallop for the doctor, the chambermaid to make up beds for his unexpected guests, the tapster to draw brandy to revive the unfortunate gentleman. In the general confusion, the arrival and departure of the London stage went almost unnoticed, for it did not change horses at this modest hostelry.

The major did not realize for some minutes that the young lady had departed on the stage. He had not thanked her properly, and he did not know her name, but he was too much occupied with Bernard to spare her more than the briefest thought.

She, on the other hand, had little else to distract her mind. Squashed between a stout haberdasher and a stouter farmer's wife, Rowena could not see out of the coach window. She did not want to think about her destination. It was much pleasanter to daydream about the handsome young gentleman she had met at the Four Feathers.

He must be a soldier, if his companion had been wounded in battle. Perhaps that explained his stern face, that and worry for his friend. In spite of it he was excessively good-looking, with his thick, dark hair and grey eyes, tall and slim yet broad shouldered. He had a commanding air about him—she remembered how she had jumped to obey his first shouted order—but his kindness in caring for the injured man had impressed her more. His strong, sun-browned hands had moved with no less gentle care than her own. And when he smiled at her, briefly, ruefully, it was like the sun coming out from behind the clouds.

Rowena shook her head at her own fancy, and resolved to put the attractive stranger out of her mind. She would never see him again. She had not even learned his name, or that of his friend. A mere three weeks ago she had resolved to face reality without flinching; here was a perfect opportunity to practise.

He was in his late twenties, she guessed, and his friend perhaps a year or two younger, though it was hard to judge an unconscious man. She wondered whether he had sold out of the army. He had not been wearing uniform, just a rather poorly cut brown coat and fawn inexpressibles.

She caught herself thinking of him again and deliberately started a conversation with the fat farmer's wife beside her.

Used to daily dealings with Chillenden's tenants, Rowena had no difficulty entering into the woman's concerns. The time passed pleasantly enough in chat about crops and chickens and children, until Mrs. Peabody struggled out of the coach in Rochester.

"Best of luck, dearie," she panted, her plump red face reappearing at the door a moment later.

Her place was taken by a thin, taciturn clerk, and Rowena dozed for much of the rest of the way into London. When she roused, as the coach lumbered across Blackfriars Bridge, she was annoyed to realize that she had dreamed of riding round Chillenden with the dark-haired soldier.

The yard of the White Bear Inn, in Piccadilly, was a bewildering confusion of coaches, horses and shouting people. Rowena found a boy to carry her trunk down the street to the Bull and Mouth, home of the Worcester stage, and she retired exhausted to her chamber with a bowl of soup.

It was still dark next morning when she was called. She swallowed a hurried breakfast of bread and butter and tea before boarding the stage, which pulled out of the busy yard at precisely five o'clock. She had a seat by the window this time, and she enjoyed watching the scenery, all new to her. Nonetheless she was growing very weary by the time they reached Broadway, shortly before seven in the evening. It was difficult to avoid feeling apprehensive about the approach of her new life.

A change of horses was waiting, and the coach stopped scarcely long enough to set down Rowena and her trunk at the White Hart before it rumbled on its way up the hill.

The White Hart was an impressive, gabled building of Cotswold stone, its façade set back between two projecting wings. The ostlers had disappeared, no one was about and Rowena suddenly felt very lost and alone. Bracing her shoulders she marched inside.

The landlady hurried forward to greet her, then swept a scornful glance over her plain, travel-worn, grey dress.

"Yes?" she enquired.

Rowena's chin rose. "Be so good as to inform me whether a carriage from Grove Park is waiting," she said haughtily. "My aunt, Lady Grove, was to send someone to meet me here."

The woman thawed a little but shook her head. "No, miss, nobody here from Grove Park, though the stage were late as usual. 'Spect you'd like a cup o' tea while you wait?"

Rowena thought of the shrinking number of coins in her purse. But she was nearly at the end of her journey, she did need refreshment and surely even so grand a place could not charge more than a penny or two for a cup of tea. She went into the coffee room, taking a seat by the window where she would see the moment her aunt's carriage arrived.

By the time the clock struck eight, dismay had become a cold certainty that she had been forgotten.

IT WAS DARK when Rowena trudged up the steps of her aunt's house and tugged on the bell-pull. The door swung open and a large, stolid footman stared down at her.

"Servants' entrance is round to the right," he directed with a disdainful sniff, as if he doubted that she was fit to appear even there.

Rowena was too tired and dispirited for a display of pride.

"I am Lady Grove's niece," she said quietly. "Please tell her ladyship that I have arrived."

He looked sceptical but opened the door far enough for her to enter. "Wait 'ere," he said firmly, then added as insurance lest she was more important than she appeared: "If you please, miss."

She set down her bandbox and sank into a straight chair with a tapestry seat, regardless of her dusty condition. Taking off her sadly crushed bonnet, she leaned her head back against the wall and closed her eyes until she heard footsteps.

The footman returned with the butler, a small, stout personage with supercilious eyebrows and eyes as sharp as gimlets.

"Miss Caxton?"

Rowena nodded, glad that at least someone had heard of her.

"Her ladyship was not expecting you tonight, miss, but I shall inform her of your arrival."

"Thank you. I should like to wash before I see my aunt."

"I shall inquire as to whether Mrs. Dart has had a room made up yet, miss." He bent very slightly at the waist in a travesty of a bow and went off.

Though polite, the butler's attitude had most definitely been condescending. Rowena wondered if it was due to her bedraggled appearance, or if this was what she had to expect in future as a poor relation. Her aunt's demeanour towards her would doubtless be reflected in the servants' behaviour. Since Lady Grove had forgotten the date of her arrival, the butler had deduced that her position in the household was to be insignificant.

She had resolved to bear with patience any slights the family might heap upon her, but she had not foreseen the possible insolence of their servants. It would be a constant struggle to keep her temper under such treatment.

These unhappy thoughts were interrupted by a loud voice.

"Rowena, my dear child, you are a day early!"

A buxom lady was descending the stair in a rustle of purple satin, both hands held out in welcome. Much heartened by this greeting, however inaccurate, Rowena rose and curtsied.

"Aunt Hermione," she murmured, and went to embrace her aunt.

She was held off at arms' length.

"Lud, girl, you are filthy! Never say that you walked from Broadway? Silly creature, you should have hired a gig or stayed the night at the White Hart. We did not expect you before tomorrow, for you wrote that you meant to leave home yesterday, and Millicent was persuaded that you would spend a day shopping in London. Millicent has had two Seasons in town, you know, and is convinced that the only proper modistes are to be found in London. She despises the shops in Broadway, and even in Cheltenham, and indeed her beauty deserves something better. She had suitors by the score, I promise you, but none were quite good enough for the dear girl. Millicent is too sensitive and discriminating to accept the first eligible offer. But we must not stand here chattering, my dear, when Millicent is waiting eagerly to greet you. And Anne and Sir Henry, too, of course!"

"I am very tired and dirty, Aunt, as you observed. I should prefer to wait until tomorrow to meet Sir Henry and my cousins."

"Nonsense, child. Millicent will never forgive me if I do not make you known to her tonight."

Lady Grove started up the stairs, with Rowena following perforce. Before they reached the top, a tall, thin girl appeared on the landing. She was wearing the simple white muslin gown of a schoolroom miss, and her dark hair was pulled severely back from her pale face. Rowena thought her quite plain. Surely this was not the beautiful Millicent.

"Cousin Rowena?" Her unexceptional looks were forgotten when she spoke, for her voice was low, melodious, with a bell-like clarity of tone. "I am Anne. How happy I am to meet you!"

"So you have torn yourself from your book, Anne," said her ladyship. "I fear Anne is quite the bluestocking," she added to Rowena. "She will never have her sister's success. Ah, there is Mrs. Dart. I will see whether your bedchamber is prepared. Mrs. Dart! Mrs. Dart!" She sailed away down a corridor.

Rowena smiled sympathetically at her younger cousin.

"Do you like to read?" the girl asked eagerly, ignoring her mother's criticism.

"I read the classics with Papa. Otherwise I have had little time for anything but agricultural journals. I daresay Cousin Millicent does not share your love of books?"

"No, she never reads anything but *Ackermann's* and the *Ladies' Magazine*. Mama says I am no companion for her, which is why she is so pleased that you are come to live with us."

"I hope Millicent is also pleased?"

"She is afraid that you might be a rival. She will be delighted that you are... Oh, I beg your pardon, cousin! Mama is forever scolding my wretched tongue. I am sure that when you have recovered from your journey and put on an elegant gown you will look quite differently."

Rowena was piqued, for though she did not count herself a beauty she was generally considered to be passably pretty. However, she was hardly at her best, and Anne looked at her so anxiously that she could not resent her comment.

She forced her lips into a faint smile of reassurance. It was more and more difficult to behave with complaisance when all she wanted was to find her chamber, prepared or not, and sink into bed.

Lady Grove reappeared. They followed her into a drawing room decorated in the Chinese fashion, with an overabundance of imitation bamboo and red lacquer. The only comfortable chair in the room was set before the empty fireplace, and in it slumbered a tall, thin

gentleman. His resemblance to Anne made it plain that
this was her father, Sir Henry Grove.

In front of the window on the far side of the room,
framed by curtains of scarlet Chinese silk embroidered
with dragons and mandarins, stood a pianoforte. At it
sat a young lady of startling loveliness. Her ringlets were
the colour of new-minted guineas, gleaming in the candlelight. Eyes as blue as the midday sky, beneath delicately arched brows; a straight little nose; lips like a
rosebud, with a charming suggestion of a pout; all these
were set in a perfectly oval face with a complexion of
flawless alabaster.

Rowena had to agree: Millicent was a beauty.

Her cousin did not rise to greet her but continued to
play while her mother looked on with fond admiration. Rowena was ready to excuse herself and retire
forthwith, when the sonata ended with a flourish.

Millicent turned from her music with an elaborate
show of surprise. "Dearest Mama, I did not realize you
had returned. Is this my cousin?" The calculating look
in her blue eyes was instantly replaced by dismissal as
she took in Rowena's dishevelled appearance. "How do
you do, cousin," she said carelessly, still remaining
seated. "Do you play the pianoforte?"

"No," said Rowena baldly, then with an effort
added, "I shall be delighted to listen to you tomorrow.
At present I am too tired to appreciate your talent."

Millicent sniffed, turned back to the keyboard and
began another piece.

"The gentlemen are in raptures over her playing,"
whispered Lady Grove. "Come and meet Sir Henry
now."

"Papa is asleep," objected Anne, "and Cousin
Rowena not far from it."

Her words were ignored as her mother shook her father's shoulder. "Sir Henry, here is my niece arrived early. You recollect I told you she was coming to live at Grove Park."

The baronet blinked in drowsy bewilderment as Rowena curtsied.

"Charmed, I'm sure," he murmured, and his head nodded again.

Anne took Rowena's hand and tugged her towards the door.

"I shall take Rowena to her room now," she announced firmly, and they made their escape before her ladyship could protest.

Rowena was asleep before Anne left her chamber. If a certain soldier haunted her dreams, she was unaware of it.

CHAPTER THREE

HER FIRST MORNING at Grove Park, Rowena was awakened by a maid who set a cup of tea on the table by her bed and flung back the window curtains to admit a flood of sunlight.

"T'carrier brung your trunk from the White Hart already, miss," the girl told her. "Miss Minton said as I'm to hang up your things."

"Miss Minton?"

"Miss Millicent's abigail. What'll you wear, miss?"

"I'm not sure. I should like a bath first, if you please." Rowena had been too tired the night before to do more than wash her face and hands.

"Doubt there's time, miss." The maid shook her head. "Miss Millicent wants to walk down to t'village and Miss Anne won't go wi' her so she sent to wake you. Miss Millicent gets that impatient, it don't do to keep her waiting."

Rowena opened her mouth to say that her cousin could certainly wait while she bathed, when the impropriety of discussing the matter with a servant struck her. For the moment she would comply with Millicent's expectations. At least the maid, though friendly, was properly respectful.

The footman carried in her trunk and she donned the least crushed of her dresses, a pale grey muslin. She had never been much concerned with clothes, but she was

longing to escape her half-mourning and wear colours
again.

She found Millicent in the breakfast room.

"So here you are at last, Rowena. I have been waiting this age."

"Good morning, cousin. It looks like a beautiful day
for a walk. I shall be with you shortly."

Despite Millicent's obvious impatience, Rowena sat
down to a hearty meal of toast, eggs and ham, for she
had scarcely eaten in two days. She must demonstrate
that though willing to oblige she was not to be bullied.
She consumed every bite before putting on her bonnet
and declaring herself ready to go.

The house, an unpretentious manor built of the local stone, was situated in a shallow valley on the edge of
the Cotswolds, facing west across the Vale of Evesham. As the girls walked across the park, Rowena saw
that it was surrounded on three sides by rolling hills
covered with grass cropped short by countless sheep.
They left the park and followed a winding lane down-
hill between hawthorn hedges riotous with sweet-
scented honeysuckle.

After about half a mile, Millicent interrupted her
discourse on the joys of a London Season and the
boredom of country life to point out a short cut to the
village. They climbed a stile beside a five-barred gate,
and started across an apple orchard.

"Whose land is this, cousin?" asked Rowena. "They
are going to have a poor harvest, I fear. It looks as if the
trees have not been pruned this age, and they are all old-
fashioned varieties."

Millicent raised her charming eyebrows at this display of unladylike knowledge, but the question was of
interest to her and she answered readily.

"It is part of Farleigh Grange. The earl died over a year ago, and there has been some difficulty finding his heir. He had no sons, and no close male relatives. We visit Lady Farleigh, of course, though she is shockingly rude sometimes. She is a disagreeable old cat, and invalidish, too, but after all she is a countess."

She went on to provide details of the various occasions upon which Lady Farleigh had insulted Lady Grove. Rowena gave her half her attention, the other half being on the neglected state of the orchards through which they strolled. She mentally catalogued all the improvements she would make if they belonged to her.

Soon they reached the village of Down Stanton, a tiny hamlet boasting a single shop. Rolls of ribbon and cards of pins hung between barrels of flour and a rickety stack of cheap tin buckets. Millicent gathered her skirts close about her and sniffed in disdain as she examined the ribbons in a desultory manner. Rowena wondered why she had come here. Surely there was nothing to attract a young lady who wore London fashions.

Millicent brightened at the sound of hooves and wheels in the village street. She hurried outside without a word to the shop's proprietor, a tiny, plump woman who had hovered hopefully since their arrival.

"I believe my cousin was unable to find the precise shade she needs," said Rowena apologetically.

"Never you mind, dearie. Miss Grove is never satisfied," the woman assured her. "Her cousin, are you then? Come to visit for a while?"

"I am going to live at Grove Park," said Rowena, well aware that the news would be all over the neighbourhood before dark. With a nod of farewell, she followed Millicent out into the street.

She was standing beside a smart phaeton, orange with black trim, beaming up at the driver. That gentleman was also orange with black trim, Rowena saw with a shock of amusement. At least, his coat, with its pinched-in waist and padded shoulders, and his boots were black, his waistcoat and pantaloons a startling shade of orange. A huge topaz stickpin adorned a neckcloth, of ordinary white muslin, so high and starched that the effort of looking down at Millicent appeared to be strangling him. His face clashed horribly with his apparel.

"Mr. Ruddle has invited me to go for a drive," Millicent called gaily, not troubling to perform any introductions. "You will not mind walking home, will you, Rowena? It is not far and you know the way now. There is scarce room in the carriage for more than two."

Before Rowena could voice the least objection, the black-clad groom had helped her cousin into the phaeton and Mr. Ruddle, saluting her with a wave of his whip, had set his coal-black team in motion. She watched till they were out of sight, hoping that her aunt would not hold her responsible for Millicent's escapade.

She enjoyed the walk back up the hill without Millicent's endless chatter. A blackbird sang to her and she was at leisure to admire the tall spikes of foxgloves by the wayside. She might almost have been at home, only there she would probably have been riding. Where was Vixen now?

On reaching the house, she sought out Lady Grove at once and told her of her daughter's defection.

"I do not mean to carry tales," she said, "but I cannot think it right to let her go off alone with a gentleman of whom I know nothing."

"It is perfectly unexceptionable as long as there was a groom present." Her ladyship was complacent. "Mr. Adolphus Ruddle never goes anywhere without a servant. He is rich as Golden Ball and he admires dear Millicent excessively, but it is a pity that he has no title. Indeed, Millicent is quite fond of him, but naturally she cannot like to marry a man without a title even if he is wealthy and quite the gentleman. I have told her a thousand times that she deserves a duke."

"But perhaps she would be happier with Mr. Ruddle, if she is fond of him."

Aunt Hermione shook her head indulgently at this irrelevant comment. "Why, even I managed to catch a baronet, and I did not have one tenth Millicent's looks. And then Ruddle is such an unfortunate name! Ruddle Towers simply does not have that *ring* to it, though it is a splendid house, to be sure. I daresay they will be home before luncheon. I must see Cook."

Rowena soon learned that Millicent could do no wrong in her mother's eyes. The combination of startling beauty and the fortune inherited from the great-aunt after whom she was named set her above reproach. Sir Henry had long since abdicated responsibility for his daughters, and only Anne ever crossed her sister, retiring to her books to escape the scolds this brought her for being disagreeable. As long as Rowena deferred to Millicent's wishes, Aunt Hermione treated her as another daughter. If Millicent frowned, her mother frowned.

Lady Grove was extremely conscientious about her duties as a landowner's wife, visiting the tenants regularly to keep an eye on their welfare. Neither of her daughters ever offered to accompany her on her rounds.

Rowena would have been delighted to do so, but she was not invited and she felt it was not her place to suggest it.

Having little else to occupy her time, she had no objection to accompanying her cousin on walks and carriage rides, and calling on the neighbours with her when Lady Grove was otherwise occupied.

Rowena met the Berry-Brownings, the Thorncrests and the Desboroughs, country gentry of the kind she had been on familiar terms with in Kent. Here, however, she found herself very much relegated to the background. This was only in part because of Millicent's beauty and her long acquaintance with the families they called on.

Millicent's manners in company were charming, and the higher the rank of her hostess the more charming they became. They reached their acme wherever an eligible gentleman was to be found in the household. With such an air of commiserating sympathy did she mention Rowena's unhappy status as a poor relation that it was difficult for her victim to take open exception to it.

"It is *so* sad that dear Cousin Rowena has been left without a penny," she observed on more than one occasion, "and prodigious gratifying, I vow, that we are able to offer her a home."

Though Millicent spoke nothing but the truth, Rowena had to battle a strong urge to express her resentment over this sugar-coated disparagement. She was proud of herself for her victory over her tongue.

Unfortunately, to Millicent this silence appeared to be weakness rather than strength of character. She took increasing advantage of her cousin's compliance. Scarce a fortnight had passed when, after her usual late breakfast, she sought out Rowena in the parlour.

It was a gloomy day, threatening rain. Rowena was comfortably ensconced in a large armchair with a book she had found in her uncle's library, a translation of Cato's *De Agricultura*. She was no great reader, as she had confessed to Anne, but she was fascinated by the early Romans' curious ideas on farming.

"I need some buttons for my new sprig muslin," Millicent announced without ceremony. "The ones the stupid seamstress put on are hideous."

"I doubt the shop in Down Stanton will have any you like better," Rowena suggested, reluctant to leave her book to accompany her cousin.

"I heard they received a new selection yesterday. I cannot go as Mr. Ruddle is calling this morning. Mama expects Lady William, too, and I daresay Mr. Desborough will come with her. I am sure you will be able to choose something suitable. Ask Minton to show you the dress before you go."

"Oh, no, cousin, I fear I am quite unable to make such a decision for you." She hoped her voice was calm. "I have been in mourning this age and have quite forgotten how to shop for pretty trifles. I shall be happy to go with you when you have the time."

Whether because her determination showed, or because Mr. Ruddle was announced at that moment, Millicent accepted the refusal without a fuss. She cast a disparaging glance at Rowena's well-worn morning gown and murmured, "Perhaps you are right."

Since she did not again attempt to send Rowena to run her errands, it seemed she recognized the limits of her cousin's patience.

One hot August day, Millicent decided to go shopping in Broadway. While the barouche was brought round, Rowena asked Lady Grove whether she had any commissions for her.

"So thoughtful, my dear. Let me see. Yes, Cook was asking just yesterday for some preserved ginger, and the grocer in Broadway usually has a jar or two, if you would not mind popping in there."

"Certainly, Aunt. Anne, do you need anything?"

"The books I ordered ought to be at the bookseller's by now, the ones I read about in the *Quarterly Review*. I cannot remember the precise titles but he will know, if it is convenient for you to call there."

"I shall do my best," Rowena promised.

After she'd spent an hour of wandering from draper to haberdasher to milliner, Rowena's basket was full of Millicent's purchases. She left her cousin studying a pattern book at the dressmaker's and returned to the White Hart to empty her load into the carriage. When she made her way back to the dressmaker's shop, Millicent was standing outside talking to Mr. Ruddle.

"Good day, Miss Caxton," said that gentleman, bending slightly at the waist.

Rowena knew that his minimal bow was due not to any condescension towards her but to the tightness of his clothes, all green and white today. She had met him several times by now and found him amiable enough, if excessively silly. She returned his greeting with a smile.

"It is the luckiest thing, Rowena," gushed Millicent. "Only think, Mr. Ruddle's phaeton has broke its axle and he was about to hire a vehicle to carry him home, but we shall take him up instead."

"I have not yet been to the grocer's for your mother, nor to fetch Anne's books," Rowena reminded her.

She pouted, but doubtless owing to her beau's presence she decided not to object. "I daresay Mr. Ruddle will not mind waiting with me at the White Hart for a few minutes while you go. But hurry, cousin, I've no wish to sit about all day.''

Rowena hurried. Nonetheless, when she returned to the inn the carriage was gone. A moment's consideration persuaded her that it would be pointless to rely on Millicent's returning to pick her up. Her basket laden down with a stoneware jar of ginger and two weighty volumes of Mr. John Brand's *Observations on Popular Antiquities*, she set out to walk the four hilly miles to Grove Park.

An hour later she paused to rest on a stile, wishing heartily that she had thought to return the books to the shop for Anne to fetch another day. She was hot and tired, and her grey gown was white with dust from the road. There was still a mile or more to go, though at least it would be pleasanter walking from here as she knew a short cut across the fields.

A rumble of wheels drew her eyes back the way she had come in the hope of a ride in a farmer's cart. However, the vehicle that appeared, though dusty as herself, was a smart curricle bearing two gentlemen with a groom up behind. To her surprise it drew up beside her and the driver hailed her.

''Do you know the way to Farleigh Grange, girl?'' he demanded in a well-remembered voice.

She looked up into the grey eyes of the soldier from the Four Feathers.

CHAPTER FOUR

THE ACCOMMODATIONS at the Four Feathers had not been such as to encourage the major and his friend to linger. As soon as the doctor from Canterbury had pronounced Bernard fit to travel, Chris went into the town and hired the most comfortable chaise he could find, regardless of expense.

"I saved money on the horses." He grinned at his friend's expression as he helped him into the carriage. "I know you prefer to travel behind a dashing team, but this sorry pair of nags will ensure that our coachman does not try to give the go-by to anything else on the road this time."

Bernard snorted. "We'll be lucky to reach London this day week."

"Two days. Dr. Benson made me promise to go slow, and I think him a good man. At least he knows his limitations and did not try to take the shrapnel out of you." Chris recalled the girl with green eyes who had recommended the doctor. Her face had faded from his memory, leaving a niggling annoyance with himself for not expressing his gratitude while he had the chance. He shrugged. It was too late now.

Bernard settled back against the cushions, his face strained. "I'm weak as a kitten again, dammit. Cousin Martha will adore having someone to nurse."

"Miss Cartwright will certainly not want another guest in her house at such a time. I shall easily find lodgings once I have seen my banker."

"You'll do no such thing. Do you want to insult my only living relative?"

They wrangled amicably as the chaise crawled towards London.

It was late afternoon on the next day when they rumbled over the cobbles of Marylebone. Grey slate roofs gleamed in the sun after a passing shower. The chaise pulled up before a tall, narrow terrace house.

A maid opened the door to Chris's urgent knock.

"Is your mistress at home?" he demanded. "I've brought her cousin, Captain Cartwright, and he's in queer stirrups."

Martha Cartwright, as short and plump and rosy as her house was tall and narrow and grey, clucked distractedly over the limp form of her young cousin as Chris and her manservant bore him in. However, she proved to be an excellent practical nurse and in no time he was made as comfortable as possible, in the chamber next to her own.

"So I shall hear if he wakes in the night," she told Chris, pouring him a generous glass of brandy. "He's exhausted, poor lamb, but tomorrow will be soon enough for doctors. Bless you, Major, for bringing him to me. I've had the back room made up and you'll be staying as long as you're in town, I hope."

Chris accepted gratefully, and for the first time in months he slept the clock round without one ear cocked for a change in Bernard's breathing.

In the morning, he walked across Mayfair and St. James's to Whitehall. London at the beginning of July was hot and dusty, and traffic was scarce in the fashionable squares since the departure of the Allied Monarchs. Memories of the green countryside beckoned, but it would be weeks, at least, before Bernard was well enough to travel down to Dorset.

As soon as he had presented their papers at the Horse Guards, Chris went in search of an army surgeon recommended by Doctor Benson. Time enough later to decide whether to sell out. Though a military life was bound to be dull now that Boney was confined to Elba, it was all he knew. The mediocre income left him by his father made it necessary to choose between a profession and living shabbily on the fringes of Society.

Still, there were two quarters' allowance, four hundred pounds, waiting for him at his bank. He found a hackney and set off for the City.

Along with a supply of the ready, his banker gave him a message requesting that he contact Mr. Verity of Gardner, Verity and Plumb, Solicitors. A satisfying number of golden sovereigns jingled in his pocket as he walked the short distance to the lawyers' offices.

He spent the next hour racking his brains for the details of a family tree in which he had never taken more than a cursory interest. Only Mr. Verity's scarce-suppressed excitement kept him from walking out on the tedious business.

"Frederick!" he said at last. "I believe I remember my father speaking of a Great-Uncle Frederick, but whether he was a Scott or a Pendleton I could not tell you if my life depended upon it. You have drained me dry, sir. Do you mean to tell me what this is all about?"

"Lord Frederick Scott! My dear Major, that is the final link." The lawyer beamed at him. "I am delighted to inform you, my lord, that you are the new Earl of Farleigh."

"Earl of Farleigh? You cannot be serious."

"My lord! You cannot suppose that I should jest upon a matter of such import." Mr. Verity was shocked to the core. In excruciating detail he explained precisely how Chris was related to the late earl.

Still incredulous, Chris asked cautiously, "Is there... Do I inherit anything besides the title?"

"There is an estate in Gloucestershire, my lord. Farleigh Grange. On the borders of Worcestershire, not far from Evesham, I understand. However, I fear it brings in scarce four thousand a year."

Lord Farleigh laughed at the lawyer's lugubrious expression. "Four thousand a year! That is five times my present income, not counting my pay. I shall strive to make do. You are quite certain you are not mistaken?"

"There are no other heirs, my lord. Now, if you will just sign here...and here..."

SIX WEEKS PASSED before Chris and Bernard set out for Farleigh Grange. The ex-major, sold out on the strength of his new expectations, drove a spanking new curricle designed to his specifications with an eye to comfort as much as to speed. Though Bernard's shoulder had healed rapidly as soon as the metal was out, he was still weak. Chris did not mean to risk a relapse for the sake of cutting a dash.

Always awkward with a pen, he had written a letter of condolence to the Dowager Countess of Farleigh. Her reply was noncommittal, but at least it assured him that she would retire to the dower house whenever he chose to take up residence. His first thought had been to sell the place, for though he loved the country he

knew nothing of managing an estate. Mr. Verity, horrified, pointed out that it was entailed.

Chris began to get an inkling of the responsibilities he
had inherited along with the title.

They took the journey in easy stages. Chris's batman, Potter, was heard to mutter that it was a sin and a
shame to drive as fine a pair of fifteen-mile-an-hour tits
as he'd ever seen at a snail's pace, but his lordship re-
sisted the temptation to spring 'em. The weather was
fine, and Bernard was well enough to enjoy riding in the
well-sprung open carriage.

It was mid-afternoon on the third day when they
paused at the White Hart in Broadway to drink a glass
of ale before turning off the post road. Between the
tapster's muddled directions and a confusion of country lanes, Chris was far from sure he was on the right
track when, some three miles later, he spotted a young
woman sitting on a stile. He drew his sweating team to
a halt beside her.

"Do you know the way to Farleigh Grange, girl?" he
demanded.

"Just follow this road. You cannot miss it."

Her voice was vaguely familiar and the clear green
eyes that looked up at him tugged at his memory. He
dismissed the thought. There was not the least likeli-
hood that he had ever seen this drab farm girl before
and this was no time to wonder whom she reminded him
of. Bernard was wilting beside him.

"Is it far?"

"A mile or two." She slipped down from the stile and
bent to retrieve her basket. The effort she made to lift
it was obvious, and Chris noticed that she was hot and
dusty, as if she had walked some distance.

"Do you go that way?"

"No, sir, I shall cut across the fields from here."

"Potter, go with her and carry that basket," he ordered. "Reconnoitre the territory. Thank you, miss." He saluted her with his whip as the servant jumped down, then drove on down the hill.

"That was a trifle abrupt, was it not?" commented Bernard.

"Abrupt?"

"To judge by her speech she was a well-bred female, however shabby."

"I did not notice. Was I impolite? I did not mean to be, whatever her station. None should know better than you that the army does not teach one to do the pretty to the ladies."

"Unless you are a member of Beau Douro's staff. I believe Wellington would collect a harem in the middle of the Sahara, and without lifting a finger."

"True." Chris laughed, then frowned. "Do you think the girl—or should I say young lady?—was offended? Surely she must be grateful for help in carrying her basket at least."

"Except that you did not ask her if she desired the escort of an ex-soldier unknown to her."

"Oh, Lord, I see what you mean. Dammit, I can see civilian life is more complicated than I had supposed."

"I should not worry if I were you. I daresay an earl is permitted to ride roughshod over his subordinates just like a major."

"Earl! I still cannot grow used to the idea."

"I've noticed that whenever you are addressed as 'your lordship' you look around to see who is behind you," said Bernard with a grin.

"Do I? I shall have to break myself of the habit or Lady Farleigh will think a changeling has inherited her husband's title. You know, it's odd, but I'm certain I've seen her before.''

''Lady Farleigh?''

''No, your 'well-bred female.' Those translucent eyes . . .''

''Now don't start waxing poetic, old chap, or I shall think you are coming down with a fever.''

''YOUR MASTER IS EXCESSIVELY high-handed!'' said the 'well-bred female' with considerable indignation, staring after the curricle.

''Beg pardon, miss. I'm that used to taking orders from the major, I didn't think afore I hopped down. You won't want a stranger walking with you.''

Rowena turned an appraising glance on the manservant. ''I ought not, certainly. On the other hand, my basket is horridly heavy.''

The man drew himself up and saluted smartly. ''Corporal Potter at your orders, miss.'' He grinned a gap-toothed grin. ''Ex-corporal Potter, I should say. So now you knows who I am, let me take that.'' He reached for the basket. ''Why, 'tis no heavier nor a feather to an old campaigner like meself.''

''I did not think it so heavy until I had carried it a few miles,'' she retorted, accepting his steadying hand as she climbed the stile. She liked the look of his open, weathered face. ''I'm pleased to make your acquaintance, ex-corporal, but I must enquire as to the identity of your master.''

''Major Scott, miss, of the Second Dragoons, and that's Captain Cartwright along of him. Leastways, major he was. Lord Farleigh's his rightful handle now, but he ain't no more used to it than I am, and that's a fact.''

"The missing heir! I have heard of nothing else since I came here. He has been overseas with the army, I take it?"

"Aye, miss, acrost the Peninsula and into France. He's a right 'un, the major. The men'd follow him through hell and back, and did too, many a time. Got a sharp tongue on him but he looked out for us like his own family. Look at the way he's took care of the captain. Bought his at Toulouse, the captain did, and he ain't right yet." Potter shook his head sadly, then brightened. "Still and all, he ain't stuck his spoon in the wall yet. That where you live, miss?"

Topping a rise, they looked down on the house in its valley.

"Yes, that's Grove Park. Since you were ordered to reconnoitre, I shall tell you that it is the seat of Sir Henry Grove, who has two daughters of marriageable age."

"Ho, it weren't marriage the major was thinking of, miss. Never was in the petticoat line much, begging your pardon."

"Now he is an earl, he must think of the succession. And my cousin is both beautiful and well dowered. Thank you for carrying my basket, ex-corporal. Will you go round to the kitchen and take a glass of ale?"

"Thank you, miss, but us Peninsula men always looks for a billet first. This Farleigh Grange, it'll be down thataway?"

Rowena explained how to find the earl's mansion and watched the stocky servant march off at a soldier's steady pace. As she turned towards the house, she wondered why she had made a point of mentioning Millicent's suitability as a bride.

Perhaps it was because Lord Farleigh had so obviously dismissed herself as of no account. Kind to his friend he might be, but his manners were shocking. He deserved Millicent.

She had to admit that his total lack of recognition rankled.

She went into the house by a side door and slipped up to her chamber to change and wash off the dust. Anne met her on the landing, followed her into her room and flopped on her bed.

"You look as if you rolled all the way home. That cat Millie claims she waited an age for you, so I take it she deserted you?"

"Yes. Here are your books, and I hope they are good, for they weighed a ton. Help me with these buttons, there's a dear. I'm exhausted. Oh, drat, there's no water in the ewer."

"There's plenty in mine. I'll fetch it. Minton will be furious at the state of your dress, there's no need to upset her by ringing for her, too."

If Millicent's abigail resented waiting on Anne and Rowena, Rowena equally resented the stratagems necessary to avoid arousing the woman's ire. She reminded herself that she was a poor relation—but Anne was not.

"Nonsense," she said sharply. "Aunt Hermione has told her to wait on both of us and it is the outside of enough that you should be obliged to carry a heavy ewer. Ring the bell, Anne. You can leave before she comes if you wish."

"Not I." Anne sounded pleased. "You know I am never afraid of an altercation, I merely did not want to involve you in the unpleasantness. It is past time you stood up for yourself and I shall stay to encourage you."

The sour-faced maid appeared with remarkable promptness, explained by her first words. "What is it?" she asked testily. "I'm busy with Miss Millicent's things."

"Hot water, if you please, Minton," Rowena requested.

"At this time of day? I don't know what Cook will say, I'm sure. Lor, what have you been doing with that dress?"

"I expect you will manage to clean it, after fetching my hot water. That will be all, thank you, Minton."

She braved the abigail's glare with quiet dignity. The woman seemed to find her calmness intimidating, for she bobbed a curtsy, muttered, "Yes, miss," and departed with the soiled dress. A few minutes later the chambermaid appeared with a steaming jug.

Rowena laughed. "Honours even, I think," she said philosophically.

Rowena poured the water into the basin with its pink rosebuds, and washed her face and arms. In many ways she was lucky. Her chamber was as pleasant as Anne's, if less magnificent than Millicent's. Her uncle treated her with the same negligent kindness as he did his daughters, and her aunt was all complaisance as long as she did Millicent's bidding.

As always, she came to the conclusion that the sooner her elder cousin married the better. She cared not a farthing whether Mr. Adolphus Ruddle or the new earl was the lucky man.

"What shall you wear?" Anne was studying the contents of her wardrobe. "You must be as tired of grey as I am of white. When did you say you are out of mourning?"

"Next month. It seems like years since Papa died."

"Do you miss him terribly? Here, wear the muslin with the white ruffles. It is the best of them."

"They are all growing shabby, I know. Yes, I miss Papa, but I am ashamed to say that I miss Chillenden more."

"It was your whole life, wasn't it? I imagine you must feel as I should if I were forbidden ever to read again."

Rowena hugged her cousin. "Having you for a friend makes up for a good deal. I never had a real friend before. There, just let me do my hair and I shall be ready to go down. I have some news which will please Millie. You will never guess whom I met on my way home."

"On the road from Broadway? I cannot imagine."

"Lord Farleigh, the new earl. He asked me the way to the Grange. And the extraordinary thing is that I have met him before." As she brushed the dust out of her hair and pinned it up again, she described the brief encounter at the Four Feathers and relayed what Potter had said about his master.

"He sounds interesting," said Anne approvingly.

"As to that, I cannot say. His kindness to his friend is impossible to deny but his manner is imperious, to say the least."

"He is used to commanding troops, after all. I hope he will be willing to tell me about Portugal and Spain."

They went downstairs together, but Anne escaped into the library. Rowena headed for the morning parlour, a comfortable room used by the family during the day in preference to the exotic stiffness of the Chinese drawing room. She found Lady Grove languidly knotting a fringe while Millicent leafed through the latest issue of *Ackermann's* fashion magazine.

"There you are at last, child!" Aunt Hermione exclaimed. "I was quite worried about you, I declare."

"I waited at the White Hart for hours," Millicent complained. "You should have told me you meant to go off on your own."

Heartened by her encounter with Minton, Rowena objected.

"You knew I had to fetch Anne's books, and I was not gone more than fifteen minutes. I gave the ginger to Mrs. Davis for Cook, Aunt Hermione."

"Thank you, my dear."

Millicent had the grace to look abashed. "Well, it seemed a long time," she said in self-defence. "Mr. Ruddle was in a hurry."

Her mother turned to her in surprise. "Why, I quite thought you had waited at least an hour. Poor Rowena must have been in quite a puzzle to find you gone."

Even this mild hint of disapproval brought signs of gathering stormclouds to Millicent's brow. Aunt Hermione looked uneasy, and Rowena hastened to intervene with a mention of her meeting on the road.

"Lord Farleigh?" cried her cousin eagerly. "Why did you not tell us at once? What is he like?"

"He was a soldier until recently; a major, I collect."

"How do you know that? I thought you merely told him the way."

"He kindly had his servant carry my basket home. It was heavy."

A fleeting expression of guilt crossed Millicent's face, though her words expressed only curiosity. "But what does he look like? Is he young? I hope he has received no disfiguring wound."

"He is thirty perhaps, no older. His hair is dark, and I daresay you might call him handsome."

"Thirty and handsome and an earl! Mama, it is an age since we called on Lady Farleigh. She will think us neglectful."

"Oh, dear, such a disagreeable woman. And perhaps your papa ought to present himself to the earl first?"

"Fustian! No one will suppose that we know of his arrival already, so it will be perfectly proper to call. It is too late today since Rowena dawdled so, but we must go tomorrow morning. Ring the bell for Minton, Rowena. I shall go up and decide what to wear."

CHAPTER FIVE

"TO THINK I WAS AFRAID bringing a guest might inconvenience the household! I daresay I could have invited half the regiment."

The name Grange had a homely sound, and Chris was unprepared for the mansion that awaited him when he turned in through the gates. Half hidden by a pillared portico, the massive central block was topped by a dome, while on each side lower wings sported arches, parapets and cupolas. There was an air of newness about the building, every line clean cut with no evidence of weathering. He drew up his horses and stared at his inheritance.

"I'd say your predecessor must have built it," Bernard said. "It looks like one of Adam's designs."

"It's a great deal too grand for a simple soldier. I am quaking in my shoes at the thought of meeting Lady Farleigh."

The imposing butler—*his* butler, Chris reminded himself—ushered the gentlemen into a magnificent drawing room, all gold and green. The dowager countess, a tiny, white-haired lady, was ensconced in a wing chair with her feet on a footstool. Her bright eyes took in at a glance Bernard's limp and his pale face.

"Off to bed with you this instant, young man." She waved her ebony cane in an imperious gesture. "Diggory, a footman to help the captain up the stair and he will dine in his room this evening." As Bernard grinned, saluted and obediently withdrew, she turned her attention to Chris. "Come and sit down. No, not there, opposite where I can see you without twisting my neck. So you are my husband's heir. Hmm, a well set up fellow. You can always tell an army man by his carriage. Well, have you nothing to say for yourself?"

"How do you do, ma'am?" said Chris, unable to hide an amused smile. "I am delighted to make your acquaintance."

"Pah, I hope you have more in your head than polite nothings, Major. Tell me precisely what is wrong with your friend, for your letter was not explicit."

Chris found himself involved in a discussion of the daily regimen that would best suit Bernard. It was not at all what he had expected of his first encounter with Lady Farleigh. He soon discovered that beneath her tartness was a fund of kindness and common sense. He liked her.

IT WAS CLOSE TO ELEVEN the next morning when Lord Farleigh returned to the house after a solitary ride about his estate. He left El Cid crunching a windfall apple in the stables. Entering by a back door, he reached the entrance hall just as Diggory admitted a plump lady in a purple bonnet adorned with a bunch of grapes and no fewer than five ostrich plumes. He made a move to retreat before he was seen. Then he caught sight of the vision following the owner of the bonnet.

Golden ringlets, eyes of heavenly blue, lips made for kissing and a slender figure rounded in all the right places. Chris stepped forward and bowed.

"Allow me to present myself," he said. "I am Farleigh."

Diggory swung round as quickly as dignity permitted. "I beg your lordship's pardon," he said, frowning, "I was not aware of your lordship's presence. Lady Grove and Miss Grove, my lord."

Chris scarcely heard him, nor Lady Grove's flustered explanation that they had come to call on Lady Farleigh. His attention was all for the delicately flushed cheeks of the daughter, whose modestly lowered eyes were hidden by long, dark lashes.

"Oh, my lord," she murmured, "you will think us very ill-mannered but we had not heard of your arrival. Of course we shall leave at once and Papa will call on you in due course. Come, Mama."

Lady Grove looked at her in astonishment, but her words had the desired effect.

"You must not leave on my account," Chris said quickly. "Lady Farleigh would be sadly disappointed to miss your visit. Is her ladyship in the drawing room, Diggory?"

"Yes, my lord. I shall inform her ladyship that your lordship will join her after changing."

Thus tactfully admonished, Chris pressed Miss Grove's dainty hand, promised to return to her side in a very few minutes, and dashed upstairs. His new valet, a toplofty gentleman's gentleman hired in London, was appalled at the way he scrambled out of his riding breeches and into clothes more suited to the drawing room.

When Lord Farleigh tied his cravat in three minutes flat and shrugged into his coat without assistance, Jessup seriously considered resigning.

The first thing Chris saw when he entered the drawing room was Bernard's face, looking bemusedly at Miss Grove, seated beside him. Chris chose to regard it as a hopeful sign of his friend's recovery. The young lady had her back to him, but he heard her trilling laugh. It was as enchanting as everything else about her.

"Now how did you find out that he is here, I wonder." Lady Farleigh's voice held a hint of malice.

Glancing at the dowager's intended victim, Chris saw Lady Grove's face redden until it clashed abominably with her hat. Her eyes shifted guiltily.

"I assure you, ma'am, we did not know your nephew...cousin...Lord Farleigh had arrived. Indeed, I was unaware that the heir had been found. Such a relief it must be to you to have a gentleman in the house again...two gentlemen... Millicent said..." She caught her daughter's eye. "Or no, of course she didn't. The weather is very pleasant for the time of year, is it not?"

Amused and not a little flattered, Chris realized that Miss Grove had somehow got wind of his arrival and coerced her mother into calling at the Grange. To repay the beauty for her effort, he set himself to entertain her for the remaining twenty minutes of the visit.

Since she greeted his every word with breathless delight and laughed at his weakest witticisms, this was not difficult. It was gratifying that his lack of practice at pleasing young ladies was no hindrance. When she left, he escorted her and her mother to the door and kissed her hand warmly.

"Hermione Grove is a widgeon," snapped Lady Farleigh as he returned to the drawing room, "and that chit has her wrapped completely around her little finger. I suppose we may expect an endless stream of gawkers now that the word is out."

"If so, I beg you will not tire yourself with receiving them, ma'am. If I am not at home, I shall satisfy their curiosity by returning their calls as soon as maybe."

"Nonsense, Major. I daresay it will afford me considerable amusement, so long as I am not expected to stir from my chair. By the way, I hear you sent for Deakins."

"Deakins? Oh, yes, the bailiff. I understand he went to Manchester on business and is not expected back until the day after tomorrow. I have much to learn and the sooner I start the better."

"Admirable. Farleigh paid too little attention to the estate, being more interested in building."

"To magnificent effect, ma'am," Bernard put in, indicating with his good arm the splendid room, and the mansion beyond.

Chris nodded agreement, but he could not help wondering just how much damage the late earl's neglect of his land had left for his heir to mend.

In the middle of the afternoon a groom arrived from Grove Park, with an invitation to dinner on the following day.

"Vulgar woman," snorted Lady Farleigh. "As if being first to meet you were not a fine enough feather in her cap, she must needs be first to entertain you also."

"Do you care to go, ma'am?" Chris looked forward to the opportunity of seeing Miss Grove again.

"Certainly not! I never go out, as Hermione Grove is well aware. At least she has enough sense of propriety to address the invitation to me, but that need not stop you, of course."

"I believe I shall go, then. It must be an object with me to avoid offending my neighbours."

Bernard was resting in his chamber. Chris went up to convey the invitation, though he did not think his friend strong enough for an evening party.

"You mean to accept?" Bernard sat up, his thin face brightening. "I cannot wait to see the beauty again."

"I had hoped to leave you behind. Miss Grove will not look at me when there is a wounded war hero to cosset."

"It will be good for you to have a rival. I shall do, Chris, truly. Dr. Bidwell told me I must exert myself to recover my strength, and since you insisted on bringing him from Broadway to look me over, you must abide by his word. You cannot keep me wrapped in cotton for ever."

"He seemed competent. Very well, come then if you are quite sure, but if I catch you casting sheep's eyes at the young lady, we shall leave early."

"Devil a bit! I give you fair warning that I mean to cut you out if I can."

"What, marriage?" Chris laughed. "I had not thought so far."

Bernard lay back against the pillows, looking sheepish. "No, of course not. The notion had not crossed my mind. But be careful, for I'll wager it's crossed Lady Grove's if not her daughter's. You're a good catch now, my boy!"

ROWENA PREPARED for the dinner party with unusual care. Though her wardrobe had not miraculously grown, she managed with Anne's aid to put up her hair in a more elaborate coiffure instead of simply tying it back with a ribbon. Three honey-brown ringlets fell from a securely pinned topknot to caress her shoulders. It was a pity that the shoulders were, as usual, clad in grey muslin.

It was scarcely worth the effort, she thought as she and Anne went down to the drawing room. If the earl had dismissed her before, he was unlikely even to glance at her when Millicent was in the same room.

If he took no notice of her, she would take no notice of him!

The vicar and his wife and the curate, a painfully shy young man with a prominent Adam's apple, had been invited to make up the numbers.

"In a vain attempt to make it less obvious that Millie is casting out lures to the earl," as Anne had said, to her sister's fury. "That's the only reason I am being permitted to escape from the schoolroom for once."

In her white muslin, with her dark hair pulled back, she looked like a schoolgirl. She was no more competition for Millicent than Rowena was.

The two of them attempted to entertain the curate, a task made difficult by his bashfulness and complicated by his blatant admiration of Millicent. He could not take his eyes off her as she paced to and fro, waiting for the guest of honour.

"Like a panther lying in wait," Anne murmured.

Voices were heard in the hall and Millicent hurriedly adopted an elegant pose on a crocodile-legged sofa. The butler announced the Earl of Farleigh and Captain Cartwright. Rowena noted his lordship's glance of warm admiration for Millicent as he advanced to make his bow to Sir Henry and Lady Grove. Disgusted, she turned her attention to his companion.

The captain was limping slightly and his arm was supported in a sling. He was very thin and his cheeks were pale, but at least he was conscious and not, as he had been the first time she saw him, bleeding. Of course he had been with the earl in the curricle the other day, though she had scarce noticed him. His bow was awkward, in contrast to the military precision of his friend's.

"He is the one I told you about," Rowena whispered to Anne. "He was injured fighting Napoleon."

Anne's eyes gleamed. "I shall ask *him* about the Peninsula, instead of Lord Farleigh. He won't be able to get away."

Rowena laughed. At the sound, the gentlemen turned from Millicent, looking ridiculously surprised to see anyone else was present. A glimmer of recognition crossed the earl's face and he stepped forward.

"Have I the honour of your acquaintance?" he asked uncertainly.

Millicent frowned and tapped her foot in vexation as her mother performed the introductions. After an exchange of courtesies, Captain Cartwright returned to the beauty, but Lord Farleigh addressed Rowena.

"We met two days since, did we not, Miss Caxton? Potter told me you lived here. I must humbly apologize for mistaking you for a servant. Being more perceptive, Bernard rang a peal over me."

His rueful grin won her forgiveness at once.

"Pray think nothing of it, my lord. It is not the first time. I am delighted to see your friend so much improved."

"Not the first time? I knew I had seen you before! It was you who helped me care for him at the inn, wasn't it? That wretched place in Kent, the Three Peacocks or Brace of Partridges or some such name."

"You are close, sir. The Four Feathers. I used to live nearby."

"Without your assistance Bernard might have bled to death. I am more grateful than words can well express. You disappeared before I was able to thank you."

"I had to catch the stage, and by then the innkeeper had returned and you no longer needed me. I was glad to be able to help."

"What brings you to Gloucestershire, Miss Caxton?"

"My aunt kindly offered me a home." Her tone was reserved.

He was instantly contrite. "I beg your pardon, I did not mean to pry."

"Poor Rowena's papa lost all his money." Millicent glided up to them. "We are excessively happy to have her with us. Are you fond of music, my lord?"

Rowena had lost his attention, but she had seen the fleeting compassion in his grey eyes. Was it better to be pitied than to be ignored? she wondered.

Lord Farleigh sat to the right of his hostess at dinner. However, Millicent was on his other side, with Captain Cartwright next to her. Seated between her uncle and the curate, Rowena had ample leisure to observe them. Though the earl and his friend conversed politely with Aunt Hermione and the vicar's wife respectively, it was obvious that they were vying to impress Millicent with their gallantries. Millicent favoured his lordship, but she did not neglect to flutter her eyelashes at the captain also.

After all, he was an unknown quantity who might prove worthy of her attention, and at least he served to pique the earl's nascent jealousy.

When the gentlemen rejoined the ladies after their port, Millicent was urged by her fond mama to give them the pleasure of a little music. Rowena, chatting with the vicar's wife, glimpsed dismay on the earl's face, but when Millicent took up her favourite pose at the pianoforte, Lord Farleigh drifted to her side. Captain Cartwright sat down by Anne, who seized her chance to pepper him with questions.

At first he looked amused, but her genuine interest and intelligent enquiries soon won him to a serious discussion of the customs of the inhabitants of Spain and Portugal. Sitting close enough to overhear some of their conversation, Rowena was amazed at her cousin's wide knowledge.

With an admirable display of gentlemanly politeness, not once did the captain's gaze stray towards the pianoforte. When Millicent finished her Pleyel sonata, he joined in the applause, then turned back to Anne.

"Do you play, Miss Anne?"

"No, I do not care to compete with my sister," she blurted out, then flushed. "I prefer to sing."

"Will you grant us a song?"

"I have never sung in company before."

"Lady Grove!" Captain Cartwright appealed to her mother. "Pray persuade Miss Anne to sing to us."

Her ladyship, flustered, glanced at Millicent's stormy expression. "Oh, I think not... Perhaps another... Anne is hardly—"

The vicar interrupted. "I, for one, should be delighted to hear Miss Anne. Her voice in the congregation gives us great pleasure every Sunday."

"Oh, then...of course...Millicent shall accompany you," said Lady Grove placatingly.

Anne had none of her sister's graceful elegance as she moved to the instrument, but she held her head high with a youthful dignity that touched her cousin. Rowena remembered thinking her plain. She had long since ceased to judge her by her appearance, and she was astonished to realize that the severe hairstyle she deplored was very well suited to Anne's fine-boned facial structure. Embarrassment tinged the girl's usually pale cheeks with rose. The white dress was all wrong. In blue, or perhaps primrose, though she would never rival her sister, she might be passably pretty.

Rowena sighed. There was little hope of colours for Anne until Millicent was wed.

Millicent played the introduction to a Scottish ballad, and Anne joined in with the words. Her limpid contralto struggled against her sister's deliberately misplaced rubatos, staccatos, crescendos. After three verses she gave up. There were tears in her eyes as she bravely curtsied to a scattering of polite applause.

"What went wrong?" whispered Rowena as Anne sank into a chair next to her. "I know you can sing better than that."

"Sabotage! That cat played it all wrong just to humiliate me. I shall never let her accompany me again."

Rowena pressed her hand sympathetically, then looked up as Lord Farleigh spoke to her.

"Will you play for us, Miss Caxton?"

"You must hold me excused, my lord. I am not at all musical."

"To tell the truth, nor am I." His lowered voice and conspiratorial grin invited her to share his relief. "Besides, it is time I dragged Bernard away. He is not yet in plump currant."

"His indisposition makes a fine excuse for you." She smiled up at him. He was much too agreeable for Millicent, but already his gaze had returned to the golden curls and alabaster complexion.

He had admitted to being less perceptive than his friend. She glanced at Captain Cartwright. His eyes, too, were on Millicent. However, there was a slight frown on his brow and Rowena did not believe it was entirely due to fatigue.

At least there was one gentleman who was not blinded by her cousin's beauty.

CHAPTER SIX

"THE ACCOUNTS, MY LORD? I'll be happy to show 'em to you, of course, but it's not by studying accounts you'll learn the land, you know, not by a long chalk." Mr. Deakins, a small, grey-haired man with a face like old leather, sounded as despondent as he looked.

"I realize that." Chris was not impressed by his bailiff. "However, I must start somewhere. I've learned nothing from riding about the orchards, and I had some quartermastering experience in the army so I understand accounts."

"Then you'll understand, my lord, that I need cash to pay the harvesters. I found a buyer in Manchester who'll pay sixpence more per bushel of plums than any in London, but I have to get the fruit picked and shipped and that takes blunt. There's no two ways about it."

"How much?" Chris whistled when he heard the figure. "I don't have so much cash on hand. I'll have to write a draft on my bank and send someone over to Evesham with it. My London banker made arrangements for me to draw funds there."

"I'll go myself, my lord, for I'd not trust anyone else with such a sum." Mr. Deakins brightened considerably at his lordship's unexpected acquiescence to his request for the ready.

"You must be busy at this season. I'll drive over myself, this afternoon, for I can't stay cooped up with the accounts all day."

The bailiff actually smiled at this evidence of thoughtfulness. On the other hand, Chris was now sunk in gloom. He cursed himself for wasting so much of his brass in London. In the first flush of the unexpected windfall, he had spent freely on his new curricle and pair and new clothes from Scott and Hoby and Locke. At least the need to oversee Bernard's recovery had kept him from the gaming tables, not that he was addicted to gambling.

Mr. Deakins patted him on the shoulder. "Cheer up, lad. That sum'll take us through the apple harvest, too, for there's no shortage of labour with Boney on Elba and the army disbanding. Now, here's the last ten years' accounts here on this shelf. This is the current book, and this one's 1813." He lifted down the heavy ledgers and laid them on the desk.

Chris nodded. "Thank you, Mr. Deakins. Dismiss!" He shook his head ruefully at the other's surprise. "I beg your pardon. I myself am still not entirely free of the army, it seems. I should say, that will be all for now, and I'll send for you if I need you."

His lordship sat a moment in thought. It would be pointless to sell his curricle, for he would not get the half of what he paid for it. He had chosen the horses with an eye to strength rather than speed, so nothing would be gained by selling them. There was one extravagance, though, that he would be happy to do without. His expensive and disapproving valet was more suited to serve a town buck than the gentleman farmer he saw himself becoming. Jessup should return to London on the next stage, with an excellent reference and a month's wages. Potter could do all that was necessary to take care of his wardrobe.

There was another good reason for keeping the curricle, he thought as he opened the first ledger. The incomparable Miss Grove might be persuaded to let him drive her about the countryside.

After two hours of puzzling over the accounts, Chris was delighted when the butler interrupted him.

"Her ladyship asked me to inform your lordship that there are callers, my lord."

Nothing loath, Chris abandoned Mr. Deakins's hieroglyphics and made his way to the drawing room.

In the course of the next few hours, he became acquainted with a large proportion of his neighbours. With the excuse of calling on the dowager, the matrons had no need to wait for their menfolk to visit before they could with propriety bring their marriageable daughters to the new earl's attention. The older gentlemen were eager to meet the premier landowner of the district, and their sons were ready to admire the exploits of a Peninsula soldier.

"I'm exhausted!" Chris sank into a chair as the last guest departed. "I am not used to doing the pretty by the hour. How did they all hear of my arrival? The country rumour-mill is as efficient as the regiment's."

"Surely you did not expect the appearance of a handsome, titled and unmarried gentleman to go unnoticed?" asked Lady Farleigh dryly. "Every eligible chit within a dozen miles has now been presented to you, and a few whose eligibility is questionable."

"Some of them are delightful girls, though not one has half Miss Grove's beauty." Bernard, as his lordship's intimate friend and an interesting invalid, had come in for his share of attention.

"Will it be proper for us to call at Grove Park to-morrow, ma'am?" Chris asked the dowager.

"Hooked already, eh, Major? Yes, you might even go today to express your appreciation for dining there last night."

"I must drive into Evesham this afternoon. Do you care to go with me, Bernard?"

"Thank you, no, though I do not mean to retire to my chamber today. I believe I shall explore your library."

"No doubt you will appreciate it better than I. By the by, I forgot to tell you that Miss Grove's odd little cousin turns out to be the young woman who stopped you bleeding to death in Kent. I knew I recognized those green eyes, though I could not place her."

"Miss Caxton? That settles it, then, we must go to-morrow so that I can thank her."

"What a fortunate coincidence that she happens to be Millicent Grove's cousin." Her ladyship's voice was heavy with irony.

Bernard grinned at the old lady. "I assure you, ma'am, that were she cousin to Old Nick himself, I should feel obliged to thank her for saving my life."

MILLICENT GLOWERED. All day yesterday she had waited for Lord Farleigh to call, and they had seen nei-ther hide nor hair of him. Rowena was amazed at her cousin's ability to persist in the sulks overnight.

Wise in his daughter's ways, Sir Henry had break-fasted early and gone about his business, so only the four ladies were present in the dining room. Aunt Her-mione nervously buttered her fifth muffin. Millicent's megrims always made her overeat.

"Pass the marmalade, if you please, Rowena. You must not suppose that his lordship means to slight you, Millicent dearest. I daresay he is unaccustomed to polite society and does not realize that a courtesy call is proper after dining out."

"Mr. Ruddle has better manners by far."

"But Farleigh is an earl, my love. One must forgive a titled gentleman a great deal. I am certain it must have been Captain Cartwright's health that kept him at home. Nothing less could keep him from your side, for it was plain that he admired you prodigiously."

"It is not at all becoming in a gentleman to fuss so over his health. Captain Cartwright is a bore."

Anne flared up. "He is an excessively well-informed gentleman, and kind, too, for he answered all my questions. If you want to flirt with the earl, I wonder that you do not go to the Grange."

"That just shows how little you understand. I've no intention of making him think I am chasing him. It is for him to do the pursuing."

"But you *are* chasing him."

"Anne, go to your room at once. You are not to speak so to your sister. Hush, Millicent dear. You will cry yourself into a spasm. Come up to my room and I shall bathe your temples with lavender water. Anne is a shockingly unfeeling creature to distress you so."

Abandoned, Rowena poured herself another cup of tea and sipped it slowly. Why did Aunt Hermione always give in to Millicent? She and Anne had discussed it more than once. Anne's theory was that her mother was like a hen set to hatch a peacock egg. Being a plain woman, Lady Grove had been overwhelmed to find herself with a beautiful daughter and had spoiled her from the start. Pampering and pleasing Millicent had become a habit, and there was the added incentive of trying to avoid the fits of temper that could render the entire household uncomfortable for days.

It was impossible not to sympathize with Lady Grove, equally impossible not to be irritated.

Rowena was not sure which she disliked more, the way Millicent so determinedly relegated her to the background or the constant rows between the sisters. Though Anne did not ruffle Millicent's feathers on purpose, she had no notion of minding her tongue. In a way it was admirable that she did not allow herself to be cowed by Aunt Hermione's constant strictures, but it did not make for a comfortable atmosphere. Of course, Anne could always escape to her books.

That was why Rowena did not go now to join her. She was no doubt poring happily over some weighty tome.

Rowena had tried to occupy herself with reading during her free time, but she was used to an active life and soon grew restless. She wanted some useful occupation, other than trailing round after her cousin. At least she was free for an hour or two this morning, till Millicent recovered from her fit of pique. She decided to go for a walk.

A brisk breeze herded clouds across the sky, their shadows sweeping across the hills. It was a perfect day for a wild gallop, and Rowena wondered wistfully if Vixen had found a good home. In the end the mare had been put up to auction along with Chillenden and its contents. She must not think about Chillenden. She turned her thoughts to Lord Farleigh as she rambled across the park and up onto the sheep-cropped slopes beyond.

Aunt Hermione was right, the earl admired Millie prodigiously. He had scarce been able to tear his eyes from her all evening. With Millie setting her cap at him, the poor man did not stand a chance, which was a pity, for Rowena could not help liking him. There was something about those expressive grey eyes that captivated her.

She wished she dared discuss the neglect of his orchards with him. The memory of Geoffrey Farnhouse's disbelief in her capability deterred her. Even Geoffrey's father, who had helped and advised her, would have been shocked if she had ventured to suggest any improvement in his own management. For some obscure masculine reason, it was beneath a man's dignity to consult a woman on such a subject, however knowledgeable she might be. Lord Farleigh's grey eyes would turn to ice if she was so bold as to tell him to prune his trees!

Instead of alternately pitying and ignoring her, he would take her in aversion, a horrid prospect.

Walking in a wide circle, Rowena returned to Grove Park near the entrance gate. As she started up the drive towards the house, the sound of hooves and wheels on gravel alerted her and she stepped aside as Mr. Ruddle's phaeton rolled past. It moved slowly for his blacks, chosen for showy action rather than strength, disliked the hill up to the Park.

She might as well not have existed for all the notice Mr. Ruddle took of her. In her grey dress and unaccompanied by Millicent she might have been any servant girl, and servants were invisible. All the same, she was glad to see him, for his arrival could only improve Millicent's mood.

It was odd how fond her cousin was of the pompous, vain little man. Rowena did not think his money was the attraction, though no doubt it helped. At least

Millicent could be sure that it was not her own fortune that drew him to her side. Besides, they had in common an interest amounting to obsession in fashion and appearance. Yet if Millicent was tempted to accept the fop's frequent proposals, her mother's constant reminders that he had no title seemed to be enough to quench her undoubted affection.

Rowena looked back at the sound of another carriage. This time it was Lord Farleigh's curricle, driven at a brisk trot by his lordship with the captain next to him. The earl pulled up beside her.

"Well met, Miss Caxton. May I offer you a ride?"

"Thank you, my lord, it is only a step to the house and there is no room in your carriage."

"You must allow Chris to make amends for his rudeness when we met you in the lane the other day." The captain moved over on the seat. "See, there is space enough for one slim young lady between us."

Suddenly Rowena was tired of being subdued and discreet and compliant. She smiled up at the gentlemen and nodded. Passing the reins to his friend, Lord Farleigh jumped down. She accepted the hand he offered to help her into the curricle and settled herself beside the captain.

The earl rejoined them and took back the reins. It was a tight fit. Rowena was conscious of his muscular thigh pressed against hers, of every movement of his strong arms as he gave the office to his team and set them trotting up the drive. Captain Cartwright's words came as a welcome distraction.

"I understand I have to thank you for your care of me at the Four Feathers, Miss Caxton. Chris tells me I'd have bled to death failing your intervention."

"His lordship exaggerates, sir. I was happy to give what little assistance I could, and I am happier still to see you so much recovered."

"Do you not think Bernard's convalescence will proceed more rapidly in the country, ma'am? Your Dr. Benson rightly insisted that he see a London surgeon, but I cannot think town life healthy for an invalid."

"Cut line, Chris, I'm no invalid! You make me sound like a gouty old gentleman taking the waters at Bath. A fine idea Miss Caxton will have of me."

Rowena giggled. "I think you already look better than when you arrived here. You need not go to Bath. But though I have never lived in London, I believe his lordship is right that the fresh air and peace of the country will suit you better."

"As for peace, he is like to get little enough." Lord Farleigh drew up behind Mr. Ruddle's phaeton. "We received a round dozen invitations this morning. I hope we may count on seeing you at the dinners and picnics and assemblies our kind neighbours have included us in?"

"I left this morning before the post arrived, so I cannot tell. I expect Millicent will attend most of them." Though Rowena knew that was what he wanted to hear, she was a little hurt at his obvious pleasure. She was not at all sure whether any invitations would have been extended to her.

"Lord, who's that popinjay?" Once again the captain's voice interrupted her thoughts.

Mr. Ruddle, resplendent in his orange outfit, was descending from his carriage with the aid of his black-clad groom. He looked back to see who had driven up behind him, swivelling his whole upper body to avoid being impaled by his shirt points.

"That's Mr. Adolphus Ruddle. He is Millicent's most favoured beau," said Rowena tartly.

A challenging light flashed in his lordship's eyes as he introduced himself and the captain. Rowena sighed. Not only was the snide remark unworthy of her, it had added the spice of rivalry to the earl's pursuit of her cousin.

When she went down after changing, she found Millicent holding court. Besides his lordship, the captain and Mr. Ruddle, a couple of sprigs of the local squirearchy hovered about her. She was in her element.

Aunt Hermione beamed. Millicent was receiving her due, and she herself was enjoying a certain triumph. A number of callers were there to see with their own eyes that Lord Farleigh was paying his second visit to Grove Park before honouring any other neighbours with his presence. Mrs. Berry-Browning had congratulated her and Lady Amelia Thorncrest was positively green with envy.

Anne had her own court, consisting of three young ladies and young Mr. Berry-Browning, a discerning youth who had known Millie since she was in leading strings. Rowena had met them all, but there were no free chairs nearby. She retired to a window seat, to gaze out into the garden and try to pretend she did not feel forlorn.

A few minutes later, Captain Cartwright joined her.

"Are you tired after your walk, Miss Caxton?" he enquired. "I took a turn about the shrubbery this morning and felt none the worse for it. I believe I shall soon buy a horse. Do you ride?"

"I love to ride. Before I came here I had the prettiest sorrel mare..."

"Rowena!" Millicent's voice was sharp. "Pray fetch the Chinese puzzle from my dressing table." She turned back to the earl. "It is an amusing trifle, my lord, though I expect you will soon see the trick of it."

Rowena was seething with rebellion, but Miss Pinkerton's training was too strong to allow her to create an ill-bred scene before guests in her aunt's parlour. Avoiding the captain's eyes, she trailed out. It took her several minutes to find the wretched trinket, a wooden octahedron made of several odd-shaped pieces ingeniously fitted together. She trudged downstairs again.

"Oh, we do not want it now," said her cousin brightly as she approached the group. "You have taken so long we have got onto quite another subject."

"On the contrary." Lord Farleigh rose gallantly to the occasion and his feet. "I should like to see it, Miss Caxton. Let us take it over here where there is more light."

A moment later Rowena was once again ensconced on the window seat, this time with the earl at her side. Millicent threw her a fulminating glance and turned to flirt with Mr. Ruddle.

"I have seen a similar puzzle, though that was a cube," his lordship was saying. "I expect the principle is the same. Let me see if I can remember. Ah, here we are." He pressed and pulled and the toy collapsed into its components on the seat between them.

Rowena smiled at his triumph. "That is the easy part, sir. Can you put it together?"

He picked up two of the pieces and turned them over in his lean, tanned fingers. "To tell the truth, I have not the first notion how to set about it," he confessed with a laugh. "I hope Miss Grove will not be too displeased with me."

"Not for that, at least," she said cryptically. He watched in admiration as she quickly reassembled the octahedron.

"Like the puzzle, there is more to you than meets the eye. Show me how to do it, if you please. I will not confess myself beaten by a few scraps of wood."

She had scarce begun to take it apart again when Millicent called a question to the earl. With a word of apology he left her.

She watched him. He was a splendid sight in his dark brown coat and close-fitting buckskins, broad shouldered, well-muscled, his dark hair slightly ruffled. What had he meant by his remark, that there was more to her than met the eye? At best, it indicated his lack of regard for her appearance, so it might be construed as an insult. She knew he had not intended it that way. He was a straightforward man, uncomprehending of deviousness.

She was prepared to wager that he had not recognized the spite in Millicent's behaviour. He had acted out of politeness, and perhaps compassion for Rowena's unhappy situation, not in disgust at her cousin's unkindness.

The Chinese puzzle fell to pieces in her agitated fingers. In a mute gesture of defiance she left the parts scattered on the window seat.

The latest issue of the *Ladies' Magazine* lay on a nearby table. She picked it up and was riffling through it disconsolately when a page of advertisements caught her eye. Among the pleas for governesses able to teach French, embroidery and deportment were several requesting applications from respectable, active young women to companion elderly dowagers. Clutching the magazine, Rowena slipped unnoticed from the room and went up to her chamber to write some letters.

Being a paid companion could not possibly be worse than living at her cousin's beck and call. At least she would have a little money in her pocket, and surely a half day off now and then.

Millicent had deliberately humiliated her before a dozen people. It was not the first time, but today Lord Farleigh had been there. Somehow that made it much worse.

CHAPTER SEVEN

"PEOPLE WILL STARE if Rowena accepts any invitations." Millicent helped herself lavishly from a dish of asparagus. "She is in mourning still, and for her father, not some distant relative."

"I must not dance, of course," Rowena said, "but I cannot think it would be disrespectful to go into company. I shall not be in mourning much longer."

For once Aunt Hermione backed her. "A number of people have specifically named Rowena on their invitations, though they must know she is in mourning. It would be shocking to offend our neighbours by refusing."

"I daresay the others meant to include her in the family," Anne put in.

This drew Millicent's ire. "Anne has not made her come out in London yet. It is not at all proper for her to go to parties before she has her Season."

"You did," protested her sister. "Besides, I am not at all sure that I want a Season, yet I do not mean to be a hermit all my life."

"I am not surprised that you do not want a Season. Antidotes have a miserable time of it in London, watching everyone else dancing."

This was too much even for Aunt Hermione's prejudiced mind. "Millicent, that was unkind." In her agitation, she reached for the parsley potatoes. "It will not hurt for Anne to attend a few informal gatherings. Indeed it will be better for her to be comfortable among friends before she is presented to Society, since she cannot expect your instant success.''

''Enough!'' Sir Henry, who had been steadily eating his way through an extraordinary quantity of dinner for so thin a man, for once took a hand in his family's affairs. ''Rowena and Anne shall both attend those events to which they are invited and I don't want to hear another word on the matter. Pass the pigeon pie, Rowena my dear.''

With a grateful look, she complied. Six letters of application had gone out in the morning post, but at least she was to have a chance to enjoy herself before taking up her duties as a paid companion.

''Thank you, Papa,'' cried Anne.

Aunt Hermione patted Millicent's hand, which was curled into an impotent fist. ''You cannot want people to think you selfish, love. I know you are justly concerned for the proprieties, but it would present an odd appearance to keep your sister and your cousin mewed up.''

''Millie's jealous because Lord Farleigh deserted her for Rowena for quite five minutes this morning, and Captain Cartwright was talking to me for half an hour. Mama, Rowena needs some new dresses. She does not have many and they are growing shockingly shabby.''

''Oh, dear, we shall have to find time to drive into Cheltenham, for there is not a decent seamstress to be found in Evesham and no choice of fabrics.''

''It is pointless to buy new gowns while she is still in mourning, Mama, unless she means to wear grey forever.'' Millicent paused to consider. ''Or perhaps that would be best, after all.''

"Oh, no, so depressing. But you are right as always, love—we had best wait until your cousin is out of mourning. As you said, Rowena, it will not be long."

Rowena's spirits sank at the thought of her drab wardrobe. As usual she would fade into the woodwork and Lord . . . everyone would ignore her.

Sighing, she finished her plum tart and followed her well-intentioned aunt out of the dining room. Another endless evening of sorting embroidery silks and turning music pages loomed ahead.

ANOTHER ENDLESS MORNING of account books loomed ahead. Chris sighed and hoped for visitors. Quite apart from the inherent tedium of his task, he did not like the look of what he was learning.

"Why did you halve the rents on the farms?" he asked Deakins. "Let me see, that was just a year ago."

"Aye, my lord, right after the old earl went to his reward. Mr. Verity approved the cuts. I wouldn't take it upon myself to do something like that without approval."

"Of course, but why?" Chris tried to be patient but the bailiff's talent for roundaboutation defeated him at every turn.

"You'll need to look back through the past twenty years, my lord." He shook his grey head. "Never a thought of the consequences."

"I have looked. Rents rose steadily."

"Aye, my lord, and that was the problem. Oh, I'm not saying some increase wasn't natural. Prices are up all over, after all. Something to do with the war, they say, but that's all over now, with Boney safe tucked away on Elba, thanks to you and the captain and the other brave lads, my lord."

"What," said Chris through clenched teeth, "was the problem?"

"Why, I've just been telling you." The man was surprised! "Rents went up so steeply the tenants hadn't a penny to spare for improvements. You can't just let farmland sit there, you know, my lord."

"No, I didn't know. What needs to be done?"

"Now that's a long list, if you like. Put a shilling in, get a pound out, I say, and it may be a bit of an exaggeration but there's truth in it yet. The late earl, God rest his soul, wrung every groat out of the land for his building and never ploughed a farthing back. You can do that for a while, my lord, but it tells in the end, make no doubt."

"So I gather." Chris had reached the end of his patience. "I believe I had best go and talk to my tenants."

"You do that, my lord! Just what I was going to suggest. They'll give you the straight tale without roundaboutation and glad to do it."

His lordship counted silently to ten and went to find Bernard.

It was obvious even to Chris's untutored eye that the farms they visited were in a shockingly dilapidated state. Since he had not thought to give notice of his inspection, the farmers themselves were out at the harvest. Their wives took one look at his obviously expensive curricle and greeted him with reserve. As they drove away from the last one, he ran his fingers through his hair.

"What am I to do? I cannot have my tenants living in such disgraceful conditions, yet when I ask Deakins what is to be done I cannot get a straight answer out of the man. I don't know if it's lack of knowledge or a simple inability to explain himself."

"Have you considered that maybe he has been lining his own pockets?" Bernard knew his friend's trusting nature.

Chris frowned. "I had not thought of that possibility. No, I doubt it. The books are well kept, and Lady F. herself admitted that her husband took little care of the land. Only, when I ride about, I see nothing wrong! The trees are green, with fruit growing on them. I need advice, dammit."

"If you cannot get it from your bailiff, perhaps you had best approach your neighbours. There were a couple visiting the other day who own orchards nearby. Mr. Thorncrest, for one, and I believe Lord William Desborough also."

"I daresay you're right. I hate to make a cake of myself by exposing my ignorance to them."

"Not so much ignorance as lack of experience. You would not hesitate to go to Beau Douro for advice on tactics or strategy. Thorncrest and Desborough have doubtless been bred up to the business. Better yet, they both have marriageable daughters so you will need no excuse for calling."

"If I remember aright, Miss Thorncrest is muffin-faced and Miss Desborough is a trifle long in the tooth, with a laugh like a horse's neigh into the bargain."

"What's that to the purpose? It's their fond papas you wish to consult."

"True, but it will be as well not to find oneself too much indebted to the fathers of such daughters! It's a pity Sir Henry Grove grows sheep, not fruit. However, I owe them visits, and we have received invitations from both, so I shall scout the territory before committing myself.''

''No doubt Wellington would approve,'' said Bernard dryly.

THE DINNER PARTY to which the Desboroughs had invited Lord Farleigh and Captain Cartwright took place a week later. The first person Chris noticed on his arrival was Miss Grove. Not for a moment did he suspect that she had chosen her seat to ensure this result. Nor had he an inkling that the debate as to whether to arrive early for this purpose, or late so as to make a grand entrance, had made life uncomfortable at Grove Park for days. He saw, as he was meant to, the shining golden curls, the blue eyes gazing meltingly into his own, the rosy lips pouting in sweet reproach that she had not seen him this age.

Under these circumstances it was difficult to tear himself away to do the pretty to Miss Desborough. When at last he succeeded, he found that despite her unfortunate equine laugh, she had a dry wit that made her pleasant company.

He really must not allow himself to be monopolized by the fair Millicent, he decided. As Miss Desborough turned to speak to someone else, he spotted Miss Caxton across the room, dowdy in her half mourning, and went over to greet her.

''Good evening, my lord.'' Though friendly enough, she seemed a trifle wary. ''Your arrival in the neighbourhood has made a fine excuse for any number of parties. We less exalted souls can only be grateful.''

He laughed. ''I am sure any newcomer in a country district must be cause for a round of entertainments.''

"You underrate yourself, sir. My appearance went quite unnoticed, I assure you."

Chris was taken aback. He had thought her a mouse, and now it seemed he had a tiger by the tail. She intrigued him but he had no pretty speech ready to answer her wry comment. He was glad when at that instant dinner was announced.

"May I take you in?" he requested.

For a moment stars shone in her eyes, then she shook her head wistfully. "You are truly unaware of your status, my lord," she marvelled. "As ranking guest it is your duty to take in Lady William. But thank you for your kind offer."

Not without regret he went to find his hostess. Miss Caxton was an unusual girl. It was a pity she did not match her cousin for beauty.

After dinner, Chris braced himself to approach Lord William. The younger son of a duke, his lordship had aristocratic features belied by the blunt manners of a country squire. He led his guest to a library with walls boasting more sporting prints than books, seated him, and offered a cigar.

"No? Thought all Peninsula men indulged in the filthy weed. You won't mind if I take a puff myself. Well, Farleigh, what can I do for you? I don't flatter myself you're after poor Lizzie's hand after a meeting or two." He laughed a braying laugh that revealed the provenance of his daughter's. "Not that you couldn't do worse, mind. She's a head on her shoulders, my girl."

"Miss Desborough is charming, sir." Chris was thoroughly embarrassed. "However, our acquaintance is so slight . . . I cannot suppose . . . The truth is, I find myself in the devil of a coil and I need your advice. You must be aware of the condition of my estate."

"Aye, and many's the time I warned Farleigh that it don't do to put all your eggs in one basket. Daresay you won't find a finer house this side of Blenheim Palace but there's no denying your orchards are all to pieces. It'll take a fortune to set all to rights. You don't happen to have a fortune, do you?" Lord William asked hopefully.

Chris shook his head, his heart sinking at this confirmation of his suspicions.

"Then no amount of advice is going to help. You could have my Lizzie with my good will, for I like the look of you, but even her five thousand ain't the half of what you need. You'd best fix your interest with Millicent Grove, my boy, for she'll jump at an earl and she has twenty thousand from a great-aunt or some such. That's the kind of blunt you need. Now, what say we return to the ladies?"

Unenlightened as far as agricultural wisdom was concerned, Chris trailed his genial host back to the drawing room. This time, the first person he saw was Miss Caxton. She glanced at him, and the look of concern that crossed her face warned him that his own showed too much of his dejection.

He frowned. Pity was the last thing he needed. He would continue to seek knowledge, and in the meantime he would follow Lord William's only practical suggestion. He hastened to Miss Grove's side. It was his duty to court Millicent.

Rowena was puzzled by Lord Farleigh's rapid change of expression from despondency to annoyance when he caught her eye. He was not such a nodcock as to be angry at her refusal of his escort to dinner, so perhaps he resented her witnessing his *faux pas*, forgetting his duty to his hostess. It must be difficult to go from battlefield to drawing room. No more difficult, though, than she found it to make the transition from mistress of her own estate to dependent on the charity of others.

He had no right to scowl at her so. Trying to dismiss the ridiculously disturbing thought of him from her mind, she turned back to her companions.

Anne, gawky as ever in white, and Captain Cartwright were lost in a discussion of some expedition to Albania which Rowena had never heard of. She was once again struck by the breadth of her cousin's understanding and interests. This time the captain was questioning Anne, since she had a copy of the recently published account of the journey and he had not yet read it.

If Captain Cartwright was ready to concede Anne's superior knowledge of Albania, might not the earl be willing to heed Rowena's advice about his orchards?

No, if he was put out of countenance at showing his ignorance of etiquette, he would never admit to ignorance of agriculture. It would be useless to approach him. Besides, Millicent was already irritated because his lordship always made a point of speaking to her cousin. She had been furious to learn of the brief curricle ride up the driveway. It was simply not fair to the rest of the household to be the cause of her petulance, so Rowena would endeavour to avoid antagonizing her further. She consoled herself with the prospect of receiving a favourable response to one of her applications for the position of companion.

She had not yet received any response, favourable or otherwise, to the letters she had sent out. Perhaps she had done something wrong. Since her aunt was bound to be shocked and offended by her desire for independence, Anne was the only person she could consult. She resolved to do so that very evening.

As soon as Minton, with a sniff of disparagement, had removed her dress to be cleaned, Rowena hurried to Anne's chamber. Propped against a heap of pillows, her cousin was perusing a large volume. Lamplight gleamed on her dark, straight hair, a waterfall about her slender shoulders.

"Captain Cartwright is coming tomorrow to borrow Mr. Hobhouse's book," she announced. "I was just checking a few facts."

"He will never be able to hold that great, heavy thing." Rowena flopped down at the foot of the bed and hid her toes under the counterpane.

"He told me the carpenter at the Grange has made a special stand for him. He says he thinks himself in heaven to have the leisure to read and Lord Farleigh's library at hand. You cannot imagine how delightful it is to have someone to talk to about books. He is able to explain things to me that I cannot understand for want of experience of the world, and I have information he lacks because soldiering has occupied his entire life."

"You are excessively well suited to each other. Do I scent a match?"

Anne flushed. "Pray do not joke, Rowena. I like him very much but I cannot expect to engage his interest while that cat Millie is unwed. He only talks to me because she takes no notice of him."

"Oh, that Millie were wed! If she were, I should be perfectly happy here with you and my aunt and uncle. As it is . . . Anne, I cannot bear it any longer. If I am to be treated as a servant, at least I want to be paid for my labours. I am determined to seek employment."

"I do understand your feelings, but I wish you will not. Besides, I fear it is unlikely that anyone would hire a female land agent."

"Unfortunately. I would enjoy that. Perhaps I should dress up as a man?" Rowena tried to smile. "No, I fear I should be found out soon enough. All I am fit for is as a lady's companion, and I have already sent off several applications for positions advertised in the *Ladies' Magazine*. Only that was at least ten days ago and I have not received a single answer. Do you think I did something wrong?"

"What precisely did you send?"

"I wrote a letter explaining that I am young and healthy and willing—oh, and respectable!"

"Anyone might claim such qualifications. You need references from previous employers."

"Of course! But I have no previous employers, and I daresay Aunt Hermione will not oblige."

"Of course you must not ask Mama. It will sadly discompose her to have her own niece choose to live with strangers. Is there no one else you can apply to?"

Rowena frowned in thought. "There is Lady Farnhouse, or the vicar's wife at home, but they are no more likely to approve than is my aunt."

"I'll tell you what." Anne giggled. "I'll write you a reference myself. I'll pretend I'm a cantankerous old lady and I'll praise you to the skies for putting up with my whims and crotchets."

"Oh, dear, when you put it like that it sounds no more attractive than wondering what Millie will next do to put me out of countenance."

"Well, I do think it will be more difficult than you suppose, but if you insist, I shall start work on your references. In any case, you will have to wait till the next issue of *Ladies' Magazine* before you can apply again. With any luck Lord Farleigh will come up to scratch in the meantime and then Millie will soon cease to plague us.''

Rowena tried hard to be pleased at the prospect.

CHAPTER EIGHT

MR. THORNCREST had had the good fortune to marry the daughter of an earl, and Lady Amelia never let him forget it. As a result, he was not charitably inclined towards earls.

As a newcomer to the area, the Earl of Farleigh was unaware of this prejudice. In fact, he rather thought he was doing his host a favour when, between performances at Lady Amelia's musical evening, he begged for a few words in private. As Miss Barrington's harp was carried onto the makeshift stage by two sturdy footmen, the two gentlemen made their escape from the long gallery.

"Well, what is it, my lord?" asked Mr. Thorncrest testily, ushering Chris into the orangery which ran the length of the southern side of his house.

Belatedly recognizing the gentleman's hostility, Chris hastened to compliment him on the flourishing orange and lemon trees growing in tubs along the glass wall.

"I know your reputation as an expert in the cultivation of all kinds of fruit," he went on. "That is why I wish to solicit your advice. As I'm sure you know, my own orchards are in a sorry state."

"That they are!"

"I fear I have little money to invest in them, but there must be some improvements I can make without a fortune to spend, are there not, sir?"

"Money! Money can do nothing without knowledge. I have spent my entire life studying, experimenting, working with the land, and you expect to come along and learn the answers in a few minutes. Ha! It can't be done, my lord. You'd not expect me to walk onto the battlefield, ask a few questions and go on to win the war, eh? Cobbler, stick to your last, I say."

"I did not choose to inherit Farleigh Grange." His lordship's voice was deceptively mild. "Since it is mine, I consider it my duty to bring it about if I can."

"There speaks the optimism of ignorance." Mr. Thorncrest laughed in scorn. "Haven't I just told you it will take decades just to know your land? There are no easy remedies."

"If the commanding officers of the British Army treated new ensigns with the arrogant contempt you have just displayed, then Napoleon would now be Emperor of Europe instead of languishing on Elba."

Chris stalked out. Only the necessity of driving Bernard home stopped him leaving the house on the instant, thus insulting Lady Amelia and a dozen amateur musicians as well as his host. Instead, after pacing the hall for a few minutes to regain his outward calm, he slipped back into the gallery.

The harpist was done and another youthful female was singing. Chris looked around for an inconspicuous seat at the far end of the room from the stage. The only one available was next to Miss Caxton, which suited him very well. She was one of the few females who would not insist on flirting with him, and the last thing he felt like at present was a flirtation.

"Do you mind if I join you, ma'am?" he whispered.

"Hush!" she hissed, intent on the performance but waving her permission.

He sat back, amused at her greeting if such it could be called, and studied her. She was a pretty enough creature if one were not newly dazzled by her cousin. The everlasting grey muslin was cut well enough to reveal a neat figure. In the candlelight her hair gleamed warm amber, one lock brushing a gently rounded chin. Her mouth, lips slightly parted in her concentration, was soft and vulnerable, her nose sported an endearing pair of freckles, and long lashes veiled those startling green eyes. Altogether a delightful package for some lucky man, were it not for her unenviable status as a poor relation.

The song ended and she clapped vigorously, her happy smile revealing pearly teeth.

"I remember you claiming to be unmusical," Chris accused her laughingly, as the applause died away.

"I am, but that was Anne. Even I can tell she has a lovely voice, and Miss Desborough kindly played for her so that Millie could not... I mean, since Millie could not this evening. Besides, she sings English folk songs I can understand, instead of Italian arias, and she does not warble the way trained singers do. Are you over your dudgeon?"

"What do you mean?" He was startled.

"You came into the room looking like a thundercloud. Your face is very expressive, you know; at least I find it so. I daresay no one else noticed."

"I hope not. I must confess to having been in something of a temper, but I am now, as you put it, over my dudgeon. Pray tell me, since you read me so easily, is my face sufficiently calm for me to go and make my excuses to Lady Amelia? Bernard is a trifle weary, I believe, though he will not admit it."

"What a useful friend the captain is!" She regarded him with an understanding twinkle. "Yes, you look perfectly unruffled. Good night, my lord."

"Good night, Miss Caxton." He bowed, smiling down at her. "I shall take care to school my features in your presence in future."

"But it's your eyes, my lord," she murmured to his retreating back. "I defy you to hide their message."

Bernard was quite willing to leave.

"It is not that I am tired," he said as they drove homeward, "but any performance must be anticlimactic after Miss Anne's singing. She has a glorious voice, has she not?"

"I am no judge, and I fear I was in no case to listen."

"No, I saw that. What put you in such a pelter? Mr. Thorncrest was not helpful, I take it."

"To put it mildly! He laughed at my notion that anything less than decades of work might atone for my abysmal ignorance. You saw that I was in the boughs? Am I then so transparent?"

"I've known you for years, Chris. I expect you appeared your usual imperturbable self to anyone else."

"On the contrary, Miss Caxton told me I looked like a thundercloud."

Bernard laughed. "Did she, indeed! That's plain speaking to an officer and an earl."

"I don't believe my rank impresses her in the least, any more than it does Mr. Thorncrest."

"What did you say to him?"

"I traded insult for insult like a schoolboy. That's one house we'll not be invited to again."

"I shouldn't count on it. It's my belief Lady Amelia rules the roast and unlike Miss Caxton she is very much aware of your rank."

"Much good it does me being an earl," said his lordship gloomily. "I'd a sight rather be back in the army."

"Many men in your position live in town and wring every penny out of their estates to support them in style."

"I couldn't do that. There are too many people dependent upon me."

"Your wretched sense of duty."

"I shall have to marry a fortune."

"An excellent solution. And is it not fortunate that Miss Grove possesses one?"

"Yes, if I must do it, but I've no desire to be leg-shackled to anyone just yet. I shall put off the dreadful moment as long as I can."

A LESS AMICABLE ATMOSPHERE prevailed in the closed carriage that followed the curricle along the lane towards Down Stanton half an hour later.

"What did you mean by enticing the earl to your side, Rowena?" snapped Millicent. "It is most unbecoming in you to put yourself forward in such a manner in public, I vow."

"Would you prefer that she meet him in private?" Anne sprang to the defence, unsnubbed by her mother, who was snoring gently in the opposite corner.

"For heaven's sake, Anne, there is not the least chance of that." Rowena could not help feeling that her younger cousin's efforts on her behalf were as likely to throw fuel on the flames as to douse them. "Lord Far-leigh sat beside me because that was the only seat avail-

able at the back of the room. He is too much the
gentleman to create a stir in the middle of a performance by moving to the front. He had gone out to talk
to Mr. Thorncrest, you know.''

"No, I did not know! I suppose you pried his business out of him in your underhanded way.''

"I saw them leave together and presumed that they
had conversed.'' She spoke with some asperity. "For all
I know, they sat in silence staring at each other for a
quarter hour. Really, Millie, why should his lordship
confide in me when his admiration for you is plain to
see?''

Millicent chose to misunderstand. "He told you that
he admires me?'' she demanded eagerly, her raised voice
disturbing Lady Grove's slumber. "I knew it! Though
he has not Mr. Ruddle's superior address, he is a much
more splendid match. Only think, I shall be a countess.''

"Countess,'' confirmed her mother, blinking sleep-
ily.

"You oughtn't to count your chickens before they
hatch.'' Anne's ire was not easily appeased. "One of
these days his lordship will notice how odiously disagreeable you are to Rowena.''

"I merely wanted to warn her not to take his attentions seriously. Earls do not marry penniless nobodies
and she is bound to be hurt.''

"You are kind to be concerned for your cousin,''
Lady Grove said, beaming. "Though I'm sure Rowena
has too much sense to be taken in. Lady Amelia com-
plimented me on your singing, Anne. It is such a relief
to me to know that you have at least one acceptable ac-
complishment.''

"Captain Cartwright said my voice is like a nightin-gale," said Anne with pardonable pride.

Naturally her sister took exception to this, so Rowe-na was left in comparative peace while they wrangled.

She was not such a ninnyhammer as to take Lord Farleigh's attentions seriously, if their brief conversa-tions could be dignified by that term. However, she had not the least intention of avoiding him to please Milli-cent. She enjoyed talking to him, and she knew her teasing amused him even if he forgot her the moment he turned away.

What had Mr. Thorncrest said to put him in such a passion? She had found it hard to curb her curiosity, especially as she guessed it must be something to do with his land. It was a month and more since his arrival and still she had seen no signs of the simple minor im-provements she would have suggested. Of course he had arrived too late for summer pruning of plums and cherries and the pear harvest was in full swing, the ap-ple harvest beginning. All his men were busy, and per-haps he was making plans for the coming months.

She longed to discuss it with him. The more she saw of him, the more commonsensical he seemed—except on the subject of Millicent—and the less likely to take offence at a genuine effort to help. She resolved that if ever he provided the slightest opening she would broach the subject. At worst, he would think her an interfer-ing female.

She told Anne of her determination at their usual post mortem on the events of the day.

"Good for you," said her cousin absently. "Do you think Captain Cartwright was just being polite?"

"About your voice? Of course not! His manners are more polished than Lord Farleigh's, to be sure, but I cannot think him guilty of paying Spanish coin. Besides, I heard at least a dozen others compliment you, and he is something of a connoisseur of music, is he not?"

"Yes. He was telling me about the Royal Opera at Covent Garden, and the Philharmonic Society's concerts. I think I should like to live in London, with all the music, and Hookham's Library and Hatchard's bookshop just round the corner. Captain Cartwright counts his cousin's house in Marylebone as home, for she is his only living relation and he has been abroad so much he has had no need of a place of his own."

"Gracious, how did you find that out?"

Anne flushed. "You sound like Millie. I did not *pry* it out of him. The subject came up when I asked how long he meant to stay with Lord Farleigh, and you need not tell me I ought not to have asked that, either. He is so easy to talk to that I forget to mind my tongue."

"I wish I could say the same of the earl. Do you think he will cut me dead if I venture to offer advice? At least it would please Millie if he never spoke to me again."

"I was thinking about that. Did you not notice how she changed her tune when she thought he had told you how he admired her? All you need to do is tell her she was the subject of the conversation, and she won't say a word however often he talks to you."

"I can always salve my conscience by mentioning her name once or twice." Rowena laughed merrily. "How ingenious you are! You are equal to anything."

"You will be out of mourning any day now, will you not? And it is such a waste of all these parties to go about in grey and white! I must remind Mama that she agreed we should have new gowns."

"Pray do not, Anne. I have no money to buy clothes, and I do not care to beg for more charity than I must accept perforce. You must ask for yourself, of course."

"She will just buy me more white. Even Millie had to wear white the first year she was out, only it became her, as everything does. But I do not care so much for myself—I want you to have pretty dresses. If I spoke to Mama, you need have nothing to do with it."

Rowena remained adamant. Despite her efforts, Anne had not succeeded in changing her mind when the evening of the next entertainment arrived. It was to be a harvest supper at the Berry-Brownings'. This was an annual event at which many of the county guests appeared in what they conceived to be peasant costume, while the farm workers and their families celebrated at a respectful distance in a barn.

The Berry-Brownings' ballroom was decorated with sheaves of wheat, baskets of rosy apples and golden pears, and garlands of autumn leaves. It reminded Rowena of harvest celebrations at home, and she was suddenly overwhelmed by a wave of homesickness. She found a quiet corner, half hidden by a display of succulent fruit, and sat down on one of the rustic benches there to watch her cousins twirl down the set of a country dance.

In two days it would be the anniversary of Papa's death. Her period of formal mourning was about to end; convention would once again permit her to dress in her favourite green and join in the dancing. The prospect had no power to cheer her.

Papa would still be gone, Pinkie far away and she would still be a poor relation or at best a paid companion.

"You look as if you are about to fall victim to the blue devils, Miss Caxton." Captain Cartwright smiled down at her kindly. "May I join you? The dictates of convention are hard on a pretty young girl who longs to be dancing."

"I do not miss it as much as I miss riding, sir."

"Ah, yes, you were telling me about your mare when we were interrupted. Surely mourning does not preclude riding?"

"No, but Millicent is terrified of horses, so it was not thought necessary for me to bring Vixen with me."

"I am sorry for that. Does Miss Anne not ride?"

"She has little opportunity, but she told me she enjoys ambling about on an elderly hack if it does not go too fast."

The captain laughed, and said ruefully, "That sounds like my present speed. I have bought a horse, you know. It was growing tedious strolling about Chris's shrubbery for exercise."

"Who is insulting my shrubbery?" Lord Farleigh came up to them with Millicent on his arm.

"Farleigh Grange has the prettiest shrubbery in the world," Millicent assured him. "It must be quite delightful to stroll in it."

"Since that is not possible at present," said Captain Cartwright, "perhaps you would care to stroll about the room with me, Miss Grove?"

She looked at him vaguely. "Heavens no, I am engaged for every set. Ah, there you are, Mr. Ruddle. It was kind in you to stand up with my little sister."

"If you are not my partner, Miss Grove, it matters little who is." With a jealous glance at the earl, Mr. Ruddle bowed as low as his excessively tight purple coat permitted. "The next dance is mine, I believe?" He offered his arm and led Millicent onto the floor.

"If that man were not a coxcomb, I should be deeply insulted," Anne exploded.

"An excess of gallantry and a shocking want of tact." Captain Cartwright had a twinkle in his eye. "How fortunate that the man's a coxcomb. We need not let his words disturb us."

Anne grinned at him. "'A worthy fool! Motley's the only wear,'" she quoted.

"*As You Like It*?"

"It is one of my favourite plays. Have you ever seen it on the stage, sir?"

"Come, Miss Caxton," said Lord Farleigh, "let us leave them to their Shakespeare and take a turn about the room. I am sorry I cannot offer you my shrubbery to stroll in, for it is the prettiest shrubbery in the world."

"I'll wager you have never set foot in it, my lord, have you? I thought not." Rowena's megrims had vanished. "Besides, Mrs. Berry-Browning's decorations are exceptionally beautiful, and worthy of our admiration."

"I find them depressing. My own harvest could not make such a show."

The earl sounded bitter. She forgot her misgivings in an instinctive desire to comfort him.

"Your orchards only want a little attention, sir. You cannot expect splendid fruit after years of neglect."

"So even you, a newcomer like myself, know in what shocking condition my land is. It must be the scandal of the neighbourhood."

"On the contrary, I have never heard it mentioned. I saw for myself, the first time I took the short cut to the village."

"You saw for yourself? Miss Caxton, I have ridden about my orchards a dozen times and I still cannot see what's amiss."

"But you are a soldier, my lord, and I am a farmer. Or rather, I was." It was Rowena's turn for bitterness. "The land hereabouts is very like my own home in Kent. I ran Chillenden Manor for five years."

"Impossible. You were in leading strings five years ago."

"I was fifteen, near sixteen. Necessity is a good teacher, and I had help from a neighbour."

"You were luckier, then, than I am."

She looked up at him, trying to read in his eyes whether he would accept her help. "Not necessarily, sir," she said softly. "I am your neighbour."

CHAPTER NINE

"MISS CAXTON! Miss Caxton, what the devil is the matter?" Chris had ridden over to Grove Park to consult with his new mentor. When he stabled El Cid, he heard sounds of weeping in the next stall and, glancing over the partition, saw Rowena with her face buried in the flank of a pretty sorrel mare.

In the sudden silence, the mare turned her head to nuzzle the girl's shoulder gently.

"Nothing's the matter," said a gruff little voice. "I know it is excessively stupid, but I am crying for happiness. Geoff sent Vixen to me for my birthday."

"Geoff?" There was an odd twisting sensation somewhere near Chris's heart, quickly gone and quickly forgotten.

"Geoffrey Farnhouse." She turned to him, pink cheeked and red eyed. "I must look a perfect fright."

He pulled a handkerchief from his pocket. "Here. The water in that bucket looks clean."

"Thank you, my lord. I told you about Sir Edward Farnhouse, who taught me about managing the estate. Geoff is his son, and we grew up practically as brother and sister. He wasn't there when they auctioned Chillenden, and he just happened to see Vixen in a neighbour's paddock a couple of weeks ago. He'd thought I had her with me." As she spoke, she splashed her face with water, and now she regarded the sodden handkerchief ruefully. "I shall have this laundered for you."

"Pray keep it, as a small recompense for the...ah, garment you sacrificed to Bernard's needs."

"Well, thank you, but I cannot think what use I shall have for a gentleman's handkerchief."

"You could embroider your uncle's initials in the corner and give it to him for Christmas."

"It is plain that you have never seen my embroidery!" she exclaimed, laughing. Her laugh was not an enchanting trill like her cousin's, but a low, infectious chuckle. "The poor man would bruise his nose on the knots."

"Your talents lie elsewhere, of course. That is why I am come to see you this morning. Were you about to go riding?"

"No, I have just returned. I daresay I shall be stiff tomorrow for I have not been on horseback in months, but I could not resist a long gallop over the hills. Oh, dear, Millicent will be down by now."

"Farm talk will bore Miss Grove, I fear. I'd have come earlier but Lady Farleigh forbade visiting a lady before eleven."

"Is it so late? Heavens, I must run."

"No, it is scarcely ten." His grin was sheepish. "I could not wait so long to show you my plans."

"Then let us go to the library. Not even Anne will be there at this hour."

As he followed her into the house, Chris reached for the sheaf of papers in his coat pocket. In the two days since the harvest supper he had written down as much as he remembered of her hurried suggestions and tried to make up a schedule for putting them into practice. He had a thousand questions.

Though the huge desk in the library dwarfed her slight figure, Miss Caxton acquired an air of authority when she seated herself behind it. He pulled up a chair at her side and eagerly spread his notes before her.

"You said November is the best time to plant pear trees?" He plunged straight in. "I could not recall the name of the variety you advised me to look for."

An hour passed unnoticed.

"So there you are, Rowena!" Anne burst into the library. "And Lord Farleigh! Mama is in the vapours, what with Rowena's mare and a strange horse in the stables and Rowena nowhere to be found. She'll have a spasm if she finds out you have been closeted in here together without a chaperon, and I hate to think what Millie will say."

"We have been discussing business." Rowena felt her cheeks redden. She did not dare look at his lordship, who was hastily gathering his papers. She had not spared a thought for propriety.

"I shall not tell," her cousin promised, "if you can think up a good story. But you had both better come to the morning room at once."

As they followed Anne out, the earl reached for Rowena's hand and pressed it.

"I have landed you in the suds," he murmured remorsefully, "but I shall do my best to extricate you."

She glanced up at him. A sudden shyness had struck her as the implications of Anne's words sank in. She had been alone with him for an hour, enough to ruin her reputation if it became known. And she had presumed to instruct him, which most men would deeply resent. His face showed nothing but concern for her.

"Let me speak first," he commanded.

"Yes, Major." Despite her gratitude, she could not resist the urge to tease.

He was laughing as they entered the morning room.

Aunt Hermione was laid on a sofa with her abigail waving her vinaigrette under her nose, while Millicent paced the floor, a look of fury distorting her features. Rowena saw her expression change to calculation as she espied Lord Farleigh, and then to delighted welcome.

"I beg your pardon, ma'am." He bowed over Lady Grove's hand. "I'd no notion I was causing such consternation. In my eagerness I arrived too early for propriety, so I slipped into the library to pass the time until a decent hour for paying visits. Miss Anne tells me my horse's presence and Miss Caxton's absence have combined to distress you. We met just now in the hall. I gather Miss Caxton has been riding for the first time this age. A stroll in the gardens is an excellent remedy to ward off stiffness."

"In the shrubbery," corrected Rowena. Green eyes met grey in a glance of shared amusement.

"It was excessively thoughtless in you not to inform someone of your return, Rowena." Aunt Hermione sat up and shooed away her maid. "I have been in quite a worry and Millicent was in need of your company."

Any need of her company that her cousin might have felt had evaporated with the earl's arrival. As he had no doubt intended, Millicent assumed that his stated eagerness was to see herself. She swooped on him.

"Like a hawk on a fieldmouse," Anne whispered to Rowena.

"I cannot think his lordship would care to be described as a fieldmouse," she whispered back.

Rowena hurried up to her chamber to change her habit for a morning gown. When she returned a number of other visitors had arrived, so she managed to snatch a few words with Lord Farleigh before he left.

"Thank you for saving me from a scolding, if not a full-blown scandal," she said. "I own I was surprised at how quickly you came up with an ingenious explanation, for I thought you a patterncard of straightforwardness."

"Anything to serve a lady, ma'am. I but twisted the truth a little, for you did mention stiffness and I did arrive early."

And he was eager, she thought with satisfaction, only it was to see her, not Millie. She kept this to herself and said instead, "Now tell me how to explain it when I am too stiff to move tomorrow."

"I hope you will not be, for I was going to suggest that we meet early to ride about my orchards. Surely it cannot be thought improper if you bring a groom?"

"Not improper, perhaps, but unwise. I had best see whether Anne will accompany me, too. We might meet you by accident on our way to the village."

"I see your ingenuity is quite equal to my own. I expect I can persuade Bernard to join me, to amuse your cousin while we inspect the trees. Nine o'clock?"

"Nine o'clock, my lord."

Though nine in the evening in the rose garden would have been more romantic, it was an assignation of sorts. She hugged the knowledge to herself.

"Rowena!" Millicent interrupted her thoughts. The only guests still present were ladies and as such of no interest. "You have your head in the clouds, I declare. Was Lord Farleigh talking to you about me again?"

Rowena cast her mind back over the morning's conversation. To her relief, she remembered his lordship saying that her cousin would be bored by farm talk.

"Yes, he did speak of you."

"What did he say?"

"I do not recall his precise words. Something about your interests."

"My interests?" Millicent appeared to be trying to summon up some subject in which she was interested.

Rowena could have listed them for her: marriage, clothes and her own beauty.

"He considers your interests to be entirely feminine in nature, I collect."

"Well, of course. I daresay you shocked him with some comment about his orchards. I hope I am not so foolish as to attempt to display an interest in such masculine matters as agriculture."

"He did mention farming."

"You see? I assure you, it is fatal to pretend to a knowledge of such matters. Gentlemen prefer young ladies to admire their abilities, not to rival them. I am telling you this for your own good, Rowena. I believe you might attach the curate if you set your mind to it."

"Thank you, cousin, I will bear your advice in mind."

"It is a pity that his lordship has not more conversation. Mr. Ruddle is always *au fait* with the latest London fashions and gossip, and he talks charmingly. Lord Farleigh is sadly abrupt at times, I fear, and he dresses so countrified I declare it quite puts me to the blush sometimes to be seen with him. Dear Mr. Ruddle is always complete to a shade. How I wish that he had a title!"

Her wistfulness surprised and touched Rowena. She had not realized that her cousin felt such a definite preference, even admiration, for Mr. Ruddle.

She was about to suggest that a title was less important to future happiness than a true meeting of minds, but the moment was past as Millicent continued complacently, "I happened to mention to the earl that Mr. Ruddle was to take me driving this morning. He was quite green with envy, I vow."

Mr. Ruddle entered at that moment. Millicent went off in high good humour to put on her bonnet, and Anne joined Rowena.

"What has made *her* so cock-a-hoop?" she enquired suspiciously.

"Are not Lord Farleigh's and Mr. Ruddle's attentions both in the same morning sufficient to explain it?"

"She'd have preferred to see them both at her feet at the same time. Was she reading you a scold for daring to speak to one of her beaux?"

"No, that was what made her happy. Your plan is working like a miracle. Every time she sees me talking to the earl she is sure we are discussing her charms, and today I was able to confirm it."

"Never say his lordship was praising her to you! I had thought better of him."

"All he said was that she would be bored by our talk, but she managed to read that as a compliment. Of course, that is not quite the way I repeated it to her. Have you noticed that she is much more polite to me in company recently? I believe your words have borne fruit there, too."

"What, that he might eventually notice her spite? I hope so, for it will make your life more comfortable. Also, her improved disposition towards you makes it more likely that he will offer for her and rid us of her altogether."

"He deserves better." Rowena winced at the thought.

"Even Mr. Ruddle deserves better."

"I am not so sure that Mr. Ruddle could do better. I think Millie has a real fondness for him, and he cannot need her fortune, so I daresay his affection for her is equally genuine. What is more, he is not likely ever to look beyond the beauty of her features to see the mind within. I believe they might be very happy together."

"Possibly." Anne was impatient. "But she is not likely to take him while there is a chance of catching an earl. We must think of ourselves. Now that you have your Vixen and Millicent is less vixenish, pray say you do not mean to seek employment at once?"

"Oh, no, I cannot go away now. Not until Lord Far-leigh is able to go on without me, and there is a great deal more to teach him." She was about to disclose the meeting planned for the morrow when her aunt called to her.

With the earl in the offing as a suitor, Lady Grove had belatedly decided that Mr. Ruddle's groom was not a sufficient chaperon. Rowena was to join Millicent in the phaeton. She went up resignedly to fetch her pe-lisse, for there was little warmth in the September sunshine.

Not until that evening did the opportunity arise to tell Anne of the next day's rendezvous with Lord Farleigh. As she wrapped herself in a warm though shabby robe to go to Anne's chamber, Rowena was shocked to discover that she did not want her cousin to accompany her. She hesitated. It was necessary, of course. It had even been her own idea, to render the encounter unex-ceptionable. And the captain would be there, too, she was sure, for she had faith in the ex-major's powers of persuasion.

"Captain Cartwright will be there?" asked Anne with sparkling eyes. "I shan't have to sit there on poor old Rocinante listening to the two of you spouting on about crop yields and weed control? I'll come!"

Rowena retired to bed to ponder her own reluctance.

It was all too easy to understand. She had foolishly allowed herself to fall in love with Lord Farleigh.

Nothing else could explain the pain she felt when he hurried to Millicent's side with admiration in his eyes. Nothing else could explain the joy of being with him, the way the pressure of his fingers on her hand still lingered hours afterward. Only love could explain her longing to meet him at dusk among flowers, to be crushed in his arms.

She was lucky to be meeting him in the morning in the orchards, she reminded herself, lucky to possess the knowledge he needed. That he liked and respected her she was certain. An impoverished earl could not afford any deeper feelings for a girl without a penny to her name. Were she the most beautiful creature in the world there would still be no hope. Instead, she paled to insignificance beside her cousin.

Damn Millie, she thought, beating her pillow with her fists, and she cried herself to sleep with the earl's handkerchief twined about her fingers.

CHAPTER TEN

"Go 'way, it's still dark."

"It's after eight," insisted Anne's urgent voice.

"After eight!" Rowena sat up suddenly and moaned as every overused muscle in her body protested. She slumped back. "It can't be, it's still dark."

"It's pouring with rain. Do you think they will expect us?"

"I don't care. I hurt all over when I move."

"Lord Farleigh might ride in this weather, but surely he will not let Captain Cartwright risk his health with a wetting?" Anne pulled the curtains open to reveal grey sheets of water falling from the invisible sky.

"No one in his right mind would go out in that. Go back to bed, and on the way tell Minton I want a hot bath at nine and I don't mind how much she grumbles."

Rowena was almost glad of the double excuse of the weather and her stiffness for not meeting Lord Farleigh. She needed time to compose herself after her realization of her feelings for him. The last thing she wanted was to let him guess that she loved him, for it could only lead to embarrassment for him and humiliation for her.

She lay back and watched the rain lancing down, cold, metallic, indifferent.

The hot bath soothed the worst of her aches and towards noon the downpour began to slacken. By mid-afternoon it was reduced to a light drizzle. That was not soon enough for Millicent. All morning she grumbled at being confined to the house with no visitors, and she insisted on Rowena bearing her company, though she found fault with everything she did or said.

Rowena rebelled. She decided to go out on Vixen despite the rain and her lingering soreness. Millicent was already in such a snappish mood that defying her wishes could not make her more ill-humoured. She was about to slip out of the parlour while her cousin was talking to her aunt, intending to change into her habit before mentioning her plans, when Mr. Ruddle was announced.

His arrival made her departure much easier. As she left she heard him declaiming his resolve to prove his devotion by venturing forth regardless of the risk of taking a chill.

As she came down the stairs some fifteen minutes later, the butler was opening the front door to admit Lord Farleigh and Captain Cartwright. She paused, fighting an urge to run down to greet him. He glanced up and saw her and a smile lightened his stern features.

"Miss Caxton, well met." He handed his hat and gloves to the butler and came towards her. "You are dressed for riding! What an intrepid soul. I confess that Bernard and I were driven in state in her ladyship's closed carriage." As she joined him at the foot of the stairs he added in a lower voice, "I trust you did not go out this morning expecting to meet us? I was sure you would not, or I should have gone myself."

Rowena forced herself to laugh, though his nearness shook her. "Anne and I decided we had no taste for drowning. It has nearly stopped now, though, and I thought to go out for a short ride. I was shockingly stiff this morning."

"What, even though you walked in the shrubbery for an hour after riding yesterday?" His voice was teasing.

"Would that I had. I must exercise a little or it will be worse next time. I daresay the rain will not melt me."

"I'd have ridden over myself, if Bernard had not chosen to come, too. We wanted to be sure you had not expected us this morning."

He turned away for a moment as a footman came to relieve him of his coat. Rowena dithered. She did not know whether it was worse to look rude by leaving or to look foolish by staying after telling him she was on her way out. She wanted to stay, just to be in his presence, but watching him flirt with Millicent would be painful.

"How do you do, Miss Caxton." Bernard was bowing to her. "I hope you do not mean to desert us the moment we arrive."

"No, do not go," said his lordship, seconding his friend. "We must make plans for tomorrow."

"Yes, Major!" She laid her fingertips on the arm he offered and allowed him to escort her back into the parlour as the butler announced them.

The gentlemen made their bows. Millicent beamed at the earl, to Mr. Ruddle's obvious chagrin. His lordship, however, immediately rejoined Rowena, while Captain Cartwright stayed by Aunt Hermione, chatting about the dreadful rainstorm. With a show of indifference, Millicent turned back to her faithful admirer.

His lordship grinned at Rowena. "I can always count on you and Bernard to let me know when I am being dictatorial."

"I beg your pardon, my lord," she said with a conscious look. "It is most improper in me to...to call it to your attention."

"To roast me, rather. On the contrary, I am glad of it. It is more difficult than I had supposed to rid myself of my army habits. Lady Farleigh is herself in the way of issuing orders, so she does not notice my bad manners."

"I am sure an earl, or a countess for that matter, is as justified in issuing orders as a major."

"In certain circumstances, perhaps, but not when attempting to arrange a rendezvous with a pretty young lady. Shall you and Miss Anne be able to join us tomorrow, think you, if the weather improves?"

Rowena felt her cheeks grow warm and prayed he would not notice. "I...I expect so, sir. I must ask Anne, of course." Nothing, she vowed, should be permitted to prevent tomorrow's meeting. "Ah, she has torn herself from her book. Anne!"

Entering the room, her cousin curtsied to the earl, but her eyes were on the captain. He glanced up and smiled at her, bowing slightly, though he did not rise from his seat beside her mother. Satisfied with this meagre attention, Anne turned to Rowena and the earl.

"Good day, my lord. I hope you and Captain Cartwright did not go out this morning. I shall be excessively angry if you dragged him out in the rain."

"What an odd notion you have of me, Miss Anne! Having struggled to bring him alive across France and England, I've no intention of losing him to an inflammation of the lungs, I promise you." Lord Farleigh's tone was teasing.

"It will likely be fine tomorrow, Anne," Rowena said. "I mean to ride down to the village early. Will you come?"

Lady Grove had rung the bell and was ordering refreshments. Captain Cartwright left her and came up to them at that moment.

"Do say you will come, Miss Anne." His look was warm. "I depend upon you to help me chaperon this careless pair, who are too involved in their agricultural studies to observe the proprieties."

Anne was slightly flushed. "Oh, yes, I shall be there, but I hope you meant it when you said you ride slowly, for my Rocinante is a regular sluggard."

He laughed. "Rocinante! Well, one cannot expect more from Don Quixote's horse. Did you read Smollett's translation? Is that what aroused your interest in Spain?"

Lord Farleigh exchanged a glance with Rowena as the other two delved into one of their literary discussions.

"Rowena, pray help me pour the tea," called Aunt Hermione.

Abandoned, his lordship sped to Millicent's side. Rowena saw her cast him a melting look and then ignore him to continue her conversation with Mr. Ruddle.

"Oh, dear, I hope Millicent knows what she is about," murmured Lady Grove.

"I believe she means to make his lordship jealous." Rowena doubted, to judge by the earl's sardonic expression, that her cousin's manoeuvre was having quite the effect intended. Was he at last beginning to see that her character was less attractive than her face?

As if conscious of this possibility, Millicent addressed a remark to Lord Farleigh. He responded politely, and came to fetch two cups of tea. These he presented to Millie and Mr. Ruddle, and promptly returned to the tea tray.

"Here is your cup, my lord." Rowena expected him to carry it back to sit with Millie, but he took a seat beside her. "Will you have a Banbury cake?"

"Thank you, my favourite. I hope your cook puts plenty of currants in them, ma'am."

"Oh, yes...to be sure... I shall tell her always to put in plenty of currants."

"Delicious." He demolished half the little cake at a single bite. As Lady Grove called Anne to fetch tea for Captain Cartwright, he whispered to Rowena, "You see, I grow quite adept at polite nothings."

"At least you did not order my aunt to make sure there are enough currants in future!"

"Speaking of currants, though of a different kind, I find I have several acres of red- and blackcurrant bushes. No doubt they are in as bad shape as my orchards. What ought I to do with them?"

"They will need pruning in November, but the red and black need to be done quite differently. It is difficult to tell you without showing you. Is your bailiff truly so ignorant?"

"To tell the truth, I think he knows a good deal. What stymies me is his inability to explain, but I have shown him your suggestions and he agrees with all of them. I believe that given the opportunity and the means, he can carry out orders perfectly well, and the men seem to work well for him. We need to establish a chain of command: you tell me what to do, and I tell him."

Rowena crowed with delight. "That makes me a colonel, does it not? Splendid! Have another Banbury cake."

"Is that an order, ma'am?"

With one eye on Millicent, Aunt Hermione broke in anxiously, "Of course my niece would not presume to give you an order, my lord. Rowena, you must not speak so familiarly."

"It was a joke, ma'am," Lord Farleigh assured her. "Miss Caxton's manner is perfectly unexceptionable. Tell me, do you think this weather will continue for some days yet?"

As he listened courteously to her ladyship's rambling predictions of flood and disaster, he flashed a laughing glance at Rowena. His eyes invited her to share his amusement at this display of his ability at small talk.

"*I* think it will be fine tomorrow," she told him hopefully.

No sooner had the visitors taken their leave than Millicent rounded on Rowena.

"I suppose you think that Lord Farleigh will notice you in riding dress," she said spitefully. "You will do anything to draw his attention. Mr. Ruddle was shocked to see you so inappropriately dressed for the drawing room."

"Just because you are terrified of horses!" snorted Anne, as usual bringing down her mother's wrath upon her head.

It was on the tip of Rowena's tongue to declare that she had stayed at his lordship's specific request. She decided instead to escape while all attention was on Anne, and she rode quietly once around the park in the mizzle. She knew that horses had nothing to do with Millicent's pique. The trouble was that her cousin was no longer willing to believe Rowena and the earl were only discussing her charms.

IT WAS A GOLDEN MORNING. Raindrops glinted in the spiders' webs on hedgerows entwined with silky old man's beard and colourful necklaces of bryony berries. Vixen danced impatiently as Rowena reined her in to keep pace with Anne on Rocinante. Close behind them plodded a groom on an aged cob.

The earl and Captain Cartwright were waiting beside the five-barred gate that led to the short cut across Farleigh land to Down Stanton. His lordship spotted the groom.

"Good morning, ladies," he called, raising his hat. "What a *surprise* to see you out so early."

"We are on our way to the village," Anne responded, a mischievous twinkle in her eyes. "May we ride through your orchards? It's much shorter, and I fear I am no horsewoman."

"But of course, Miss Anne. It is in any case an ancient right of way, I collect." He leaned down from the saddle and unlatched the gate.

"Only for walking, not riding," she corrected him. "It is a footpath, not a bridle way. But you are right that it is ancient. I have seen medieval maps of this area where the path is clearly marked."

Captain Cartwright wanted to know more about the maps. He fell in beside Anne, sitting very straight and somewhat stiffly on his bay mare. He no longer had his arm in a sling, though Rowena had noticed that he used it as little as possible and that with care. His thin face had filled out a little from the gaunt planes she had first seen, and his animated conversation with Anne brought some colour to his cheeks.

"The captain looks quite well today," she said to Lord Farleigh as the groom closed the gate behind them. They rode slowly after the others.

"His health is vastly improved. I fear he is still in some pain, and he has spells of weakness which I cannot like, though Dr. Bidwell says they will pass. Gentle exercise on horseback seems to have a beneficial effect, and your cousin's chatter distracts him from his discomfort without encouraging him to exertion he is not ready for. She's a nice child."

"She's no child, my lord, for all her schoolroom dress. She is seventeen, near eighteen, and will go to London in the spring if she can be persuaded that the frivolity of a Season is not an utter waste of time."

"I thought she looked very grown-up this morning. That brownish colour suits her better than white."

"Brownish! That, sir, is *couleur d'oreille d'ours*, and a very fashionable shade indeed, straight from Ackermann's *Repository*. Not, I hasten to add, that Anne is in the least interested in fashion. Her habit was made from some cloth Millicent bought and then decided she did not care for."

"Bear's ear colour! You are roasting me again."

"Indeed I am not. It sounds better in French, however."

"I have a feeling that bear's ear is the common French name for the primrose, or perhaps the cowslip. No odder than our cow's lip, I suppose. But surely the colour should be yellow?"

"If so, you must blame Mr. Ackermann, who describes it as 'a rich brown colour.' My French is not adequate to mislead you. I sadly neglected all the ladylike accomplishments in my youth and now I am sorry, as Pinkie always said I would be. I do make an effort now and then, though. Here is the handkerchief you lent me, my lord, and the stitchery in the corner is intended to represent an F." It cost Rowena a struggle to give up the one item of his that she was ever likely to possess. She wondered whether some time in the future she would regret it, but at present returning it seemed the wisest course.

He was regarding her embroidery with judicious interest. "An F, is it? It might pass for an S, which will do very well, for my surname is Scott, you know."

"Now *you* are roasting *me*."

He grinned as he tucked the handkerchief into his pocket. "Not at all. My name really is Scott. But why do you speak of your youth as if it is past? I daresay you have had that birthday you mentioned and have attained the great age of one and twenty, if my arithmetic is correct."

Rowena was astounded that he had both remembered her words and bothered to calculate her age. For some reason it made her feel shy, and she stammered a little as she said, "Yes, that's right. My aunt was kind enough to make a family celebration of it. No great age perhaps, but too late to return to the schoolroom for embroidery and French."

"Your accomplishments are far more to the purpose, Miss Caxton," he said warmly. "What is your opinion of these apple trees?"

She drew rein and looked about her. "The trees need to be replaced. They are past their best bearing years, and there is little demand for this variety since better ones have been developed." She saw his disappointment. "Of course there are things that can be done to improve your yield until you are in a position to replace them. They are badly in need of pruning. Look at all the dead branches, and the green ones are so crowded that no light and air reaches the interior. However, you must wait to prune until the trees have lost their leaves. The best you can do for the moment is to have the weeds scythed and shoot some rabbits."

"That will please my cook, no doubt."

"You might consider giving some to your tenants and workers, though I daresay they poach a good few already."

"Will that make them view me more kindly? My tenants are my biggest problem, for it will take money I do not have to solve their troubles."

Emboldened by his trusting her with his financial difficulties, Rowena ventured to say, "If their rents are not too high, they can help themselves."

"They were cut by half on my predecessor's death, yet I see no signs that the savings are being invested in the farms."

"Perhaps they were afraid the new heir would raise the rents again."

He looked at her, startled. "I never thought to tell them I would not. What a nodcock I am! I have assumed that they realized I had their best interests at heart, but of course they could only judge me by their last landlord. It's like taking over a company from a bad officer, except that I know how to talk to soldiers and I am so confounded ignorant about farming."

"You are doing your best to learn. What more can anyone expect? Let us go on to the next orchard."

They trotted on, passing Anne and the captain with a wave. In this way they covered a good portion of the earl's land, pausing here and there to examine the trees while they waited for the others to catch up. Rowena would have been happy to continue all day, but Captain Cartwright's tired face drew her attention to passing time.

It had been the most enjoyable morning she had spent since leaving Kent, and she had every intention of repeating the experience. If Lord Farleigh was interested in her only for her agricultural expertise, he should have his fill of it.

CHAPTER ELEVEN

"ANNE GROVE IS A PLEASANT young woman." Chris led the way out of the stable yard, El Cid moving smoothly beneath him. The misty morning sky was clearing to the pale blue of a fine September day.

"She is far more than that." Bernard was indignant. "Her intellect is superb. I tell you, at times I am hard put to it to keep up with her, and I don't mean that this sluggard is even slower than Rocinante. With formal schooling to supply discipline and experience of the world for understanding, she could develop into a formidable scholar. It is criminal that her brain should be wasted because she is a female."

"You had best marry her and make it your business to see that it is not wasted."

"I am not so selfish as to chain that enchanting child to a cripple." For the first time, Bernard sounded bitter about his injuries. The gaiety in his voice was forced as he turned the subject. "But what of your plans? Do you mean to have the fair Millicent?"

"Ask rather whether she will have me. At our last meeting she gave me the cold shoulder in favour of Ruddle. He is something of a Croesus, I collect, and a better catch than an impoverished earl."

"Gammon! It's my belief she'll hold out for a title. The Grange is impressive enough and I doubt she bothers her pretty little head about the state of your farms. Besides, rumour has it she will bring twenty thousand. Surely that is enough to set things to rights?''

"Yes, with that to spend I believe I could soon have the place producing a decent income." He hesitated. "I fear her character leaves something to be desired.''

"You have noticed!"

"Her temper is not always under her control, but as she is young yet, she will learn to govern it. The chief difficulty is that I cannot like to be thought a fortune-hunter.''

"A title for a fortune is fair exchange, and not uncommon either. You will not even have to wed some Cit's ugly daughter. Her beauty goes without saying and her father is a baronet and a respected magistrate. You had best put it to the touch.''

"I will not ask Sir Henry for his daughter's hand until I can show him that I mean to use her fortune wisely, not fritter it away. I must first set in train what improvements I can.''

"Rationalization," muttered Bernard.

Chris pretended not to hear. Of course he wanted to marry Millicent, he tried to persuade himself. If he sometimes suspected that she was not quite kind, she was beautiful, rich and eligible in every way, and he could not blame her for wanting to be a countess. He suspected that yesterday's pointed flirtation with Adolphus Ruddle had been intended to make him jealous. Besides, it would be unfair to expect her not to encourage the wealthy fop when she had no certainty that he himself would come up to scratch.

He would, as soon as he had proof for her father of his sincere intent to restore his estate. All the same, it was a pity that she was not more like the estimable, and penniless, Miss Caxton.

He turned El Cid's head towards the orchard nearest the lane to the village. The great gelding was restless this morning, eager to stretch his legs, but Chris kept him on a tight rein. He was afraid to leave Bernard's side lest his friend be overcome by one of his dizzy spells.

"I had a notion you were growing fond of Rowena," said Bernard conversationally.

"Fond! I have the greatest respect and admiration for Miss Caxton's competence. There is another case of a female's abilities going to waste." Chris paused, then added grudgingly, "Perhaps I am fond of her as I am of my sister. She amuses me, and her lack of respect for the dignity of an earl is refreshing."

"Judging by the direction you have taken, you expect to meet her again today. I did not hear you making arrangements."

"We didn't make any. She knows how much I need her help and she is too generous not to give it unstintingly. Besides, she likes to ride and she is only free in the mornings."

"She likes to gallop across the hills, I collect. She is indeed generous to give up to you the only time she has for that pleasure."

Chris frowned. "You are right, I must not take up all her time. I know, I shall insist that she gallop with me before she goes home."

"You can safely leave Anne and her groom to pick me up if I fall off Sluggard." Bernard laughed wryly. "If they come."

Chris was beginning to doubt his own certainty. Was it a form of arrogance in him to expect Rowena to come without being asked? He let El Cid lengthen his pace and reached the gate to the lane ahead of Bernard. The faint tones of the church clock in the distant village striking nine floated through the still air.

Rowena appeared round the bend and rode down the hill towards him. His heart lifted, and he realized how much he enjoyed her company. Was Bernard right? He could not afford to allow himself to develop a tendre for Rowena.

He plunged straight into the question of the rival merits of sheep and geese to keep down the weeds in the orchards. Vixen and El Cid soon outpaced Rocinante and the newly christened Sluggard. Their thoughts elsewhere, Chris and Rowena scarcely noticed.

An hour passed before Rowena looked round and discovered that they were alone.

"Oh, dear, I must go back to Anne. She will be wondering what has become of us."

"I doubt it. More likely she and Bernard are discussing some obscure subject and are unaware of our absence. Before we rejoin them, let us ride up that hill." He pointed with his whip. "There is a good view of most of the estate. I'll race you."

"Your Cid is twice Vixen's size!"

"Craven, Miss Caxton?"

"No!" She urged the mare forward, sailing across the stream that divided the orchard from the grassy slope. A pair of magpies flew up with a screech of warning.

Hooves thundered behind her, overtook and pounded ahead. It would never occur to the ex-soldier to hold back and allow a lady to win, and Rowena was glad of it. Following at Vixen's best speed, she saw him draw to a halt at the spinney on top of the hill. He was laughing.

"You took me by surprise. I had intended to show you the bridge, but before I knew it you were over the brook and away."

"Even with a start, I was beaten hollow. He's splendid." She reached over to stroke his horse's nose. "You bought him in Spain?"

"I inherited him from a friend who was killed at Ciudad Rodrigo."

"I'm sorry."

His smile was twisted. "We all lost many friends. Can you wonder that I fought as hard to save Bernard as I did against Napoleon? Come, it is time we returned to the others."

They cantered down the slope without admiring the view. Rowena was sure his words had slipped out without his volition. He had never spoken of the war before, not in her hearing, for he was not one of those men who enjoyed recounting tales of heroic battles. She was honoured that he had revealed his feelings to her, however briefly.

The memory of his pain stayed with her as she and Anne rode slowly homeward.

They had nearly reached the house when Anne said abruptly, "Bernard was talking about his injuries, about his limp and how weak his arm still is and his dizzy fits."

"I have never noticed him having a fit."

"Fit is the wrong word. He feels suddenly faint, then it passes. I have seen it once or twice. He stops speaking and sits with his head down for a few moments, then he is all right again. But I do not want to discuss his symptoms. It's just that I had a strange feeling that he was trying to tell me something quite different from what he was saying."

"What on earth do you mean?"

"There was something behind his words, that he could not say outright, but that he hoped I would understand. And I didn't." Anne's eyes were bewildered, hurt.

"Perhaps you imagined it?"

As Anne shook her head they rode into the stable yard. The groom swung down from his horse and came to help them dismount, putting an end to confidences. The cousins went into the house.

Rowena automatically checked the post on the table in the front hall in passing, though her only regular correspondent was Pinkie, from whom she had heard not a week since. There was a letter there addressed to her in a masculine hand that seemed familiar though she could not identify it. She turned it over. It was sealed with a vast quantity of red sealing wax.

She needed the paperknife in her chamber to open it, and she wanted privacy to read it. She followed Anne up the stairs.

"Just tell me this." Anne turned as they reached the landing. "Should I ask him what he meant?"

Rowena tore her thoughts from the letter. "The captain? No, don't do that. If it is important he will surely explain himself in the end."

Minton came down the hall towards them.

"Miss Millicent's been asking for you this half hour, miss," the abigail said sourly. "I suppose I'd best help you change so's you don't keep her waiting any longer."

"Thank you, Minton, but I shall send for you when I need you." Rowena went into her chamber, found her paperknife, and carefully slit the seal of the letter.

Anne had followed her. "Who is it from?" she enquired with her usual lack of ceremony.

"I don't know." She unfolded the two sheets of paper and stared at the uppermost. "Good gracious, it's a bank draft. In my name!"

"How much? Who from?"

"Ninety-eight pounds, three shillings and sixpence ha'penny. The letter is signed by Mr. Harwin, my lawyer. Wait a bit." She scanned the precise, legal handwriting. "I told you Papa left his papers in such a muddle? It seems Mr. Harwin's clerk is still going through them and this is the result of something he found."

"Blessings on Mr. Harwin's clerk! A hundred pounds—you could live for a year on it and be free of Millie while you seek a position. You can afford to pick and choose."

Rowena was thoughtful. "But suppose the next thing he finds is an unpaid debt? Mr. Harwin even hints at the possibility, though he is not so imprudent as to say it outright. No, I shall buy new gowns, for both of us, and put a little aside for insurance."

"Oh, no, Rowena, you must not waste your money. I am sure Mama will buy us new gowns if we only make a push for it."

"I *will* not ask, and have Millicent think of a hundred reasons why we should not, or why we must continue in grey and white. I want something pretty for a last fling before I go to be a companion."

"To think I always considered you such a practical person! I wonder if Mama will let us take the barouche into Broadway tomorrow."

"Not Broadway."

"Evesham?"

"No. For Lady Amelia's ball we are going to have ball gowns from the best modiste in Cheltenham."

"That will take all day. I shall ask Papa for the carriage and Millicent will have nothing to say in the matter."

"You are the practical one, Anne dear."

When Sir Henry understood the purpose of their proposed expedition, he not unnaturally forbade Rowena to spend any of her money on his daughter. In fact, he pressed her save it and accept a sum from him sufficient to purchase several dresses. Her refusal was adamant. All too clearly she foresaw Millicent's accusations of cozening her uncle into indulging her. She could no more take the offer from him than from her aunt.

Sir Henry, therefore, contented himself with taking a roll of flimsies from his safe and peeling off fifty pounds for Anne.

"Not to be spent on books, mind," he warned as he handed her the money.

"I shall not let her go near any bookshops," promised Rowena.

Anne was inclined to postpone the outing for a day when she realized that they could not send a message to Farleigh Grange warning of their absence.

"That's the trouble with clandestine meetings," she observed.

Rowena was overcome with guilt at these blunt words. She had been trying to persuade herself that since no appointment had been made after the first morning there was no impropriety attached to their encounters with the gentlemen. She salved her conscience now with the thought that the tacit understanding would be disrupted when they did not turn up on the morrow.

"No, we must go to Cheltenham tomorrow, to be sure there is time enough to have the gowns made up," she insisted a trifle crossly.

All the same, she was not sorry when she woke to see a light drizzle falling. Lord Farleigh and Captain Cartwright would not expect them.

They spent a damp but delightful day in the bustling spa town of Cheltenham. New crescents and parades were under construction everywhere, and new shops were opening to serve the growing population. Anne knew her way about since she had spent a couple of years at a school in the vicinity. Followed by the grumbling footman, the girls went first to a French modiste to order their ball gowns. Then they hurried from draper to haberdasher to mantua-maker, and the carriage quickly filled with packages. By the time they were done there was scarce room for them among the yards of fabric, with patterns to be made up by a seamstress in Broadway, lengths of lace trimming, fans and gloves and reticules and slippers.

Fifty pounds might be nothing to a London milliner, but in Cheltenham it went a long way. They returned to Grove Park at dusk, tired but satisfied.

Millicent was complacent, despite having been outwitted. Lord Farleigh, Captain Cartwright and Mr. Ruddle had all braved the rain to visit.

"Captain Cartwright is the soul of courtesy," declared Lady Grove. "He stayed beside me for quite twenty minutes, though I could see he longed to be with dear Millicent."

"Once the curate came to entertain Mama, the captain hurried to me at once." Millicent cast a sly glance at her sister. "It is a pity he is so dull, and a cripple too, yet one can never have too many beaux. Anne is too young, but I am sorry you have none, Rowena. You really ought to encourage the curate.''

Anne looked anxious. Rowena whispered to her, "Even I would almost prefer Millicent's company to the curate's. No doubt Bernard hoped to persuade Chris to leave since you were not there.''

"Do you think so?'' Anne asked eagerly. "No, you must be mistaken. He only pays attention to me because he is kind, and the soul of courtesy, as Mama put it. I am too plain to interest him, especially with Millicent around.''

"Fustian! I am perfectly certain that he enjoys talking to you, and only wait until he sees you in your new ball gown.''

Lady Amelia's ball was just six days off. As Rowena had promised, their gowns were being created by the best modiste in Cheltenham, and they had to go back for a final fitting.

Two days of heavy rain intervened. There were no morning rides and no visitors. Anne closeted herself in the library, to be seen only at mealtimes, and Millicent was so petulant and unreasonable that even her mother chided her. Rowena's equable temper was sorely tried. At last, when her cousin snapped at her for the second time for turning a page of music too slowly, she snapped back.

"You do not give me enough warning. You know I cannot follow the music.'' She flounced off to help Aunt Hermione sort her embroidery silks, ignoring that lady's hints that she could manage perfectly well on her own.

The third day dawned fine, though frosty. Anne and Rowena agreed as one to postpone the return to Cheltenham in favour of riding. They arrived at the five-barred gate at precisely nine o'clock.

There was no sign of the gentlemen. They dawdled through the orchards down to the village, meeting no one on the way but a flock of geese, busily nibbling at chickweed and plantain. The evidence that her advice had been heeded cheered Rowena. Anne had no such consolation. She swung between alarm lest the captain had suffered a relapse, and fear that he simply did not want to see her.

"I must stay home this afternoon in case they come," she wailed.

"You shall do no such thing. Think of what Millie said about letting the gentlemen do the pursuing. We are going into Cheltenham so that you can dazzle him at the ball."

The modiste, a round, cheerful Frenchwoman, was delighted to see them. She bustled them into two small fitting rooms and sent her assistants to help while she attended another customer. Rowena held her breath as the dress was slipped over her head and settled on her shoulders.

The fashions of that year of 1814 were of the simplest. The sheer *barège*, the delicate green of new beech leaves, clung to Rowena's bosom, gathered just beneath with a darker green ribbon, and fell straight to the ankle in a silky foam. Like the bodice, the hem was ornamented with an embroidered tracery of leaves, matching the ribbon. She twirled, and the skirt floated about her in the most delightful way. It was hard to judge after a year of black and grey, but she thought it became her. She went to show Anne, and to see how her cousin looked.

Anne was too young for anything but muslin, and though she might escape white, pastels were *de rigeur*, as Madame had assured them. She was dressed in primrose, her spare figure softened by judiciously placed ruffles. Against the pale yellow, her pallid complexion took on an almost translucent glow.

"Me, I am a genius!" Madame appeared at the door. "*Mademoiselle* is *élégante, distinguée*, despite her youth. You must hold yourself proudly, *mademoiselle*. Not for you the giggles and—*comment est-ce qu'on dit ça?*—the pouts of the other young misses."

Anne was gazing at herself in the glass with an awed expression. "Oh, Rowena, do you think he will like it?"

"He will be staggered," breathed Rowena.

Madame beamed and nodded. "But of course, the *jeune gentilhomme* will like it. How can he resist?" She turned to look at Rowena. "Ah, very good. The wood nymph, *n'est-ce pas? Jolie, fraîche*, altogether charming. For you, *mademoiselle*, the genius is not necessary."

Rowena suppressed a sigh. Fresh and pretty was all very well, but it did not compete with elegant and distinguished, still less with Millicent's incomparable beauty.

CHAPTER TWELVE

LADY AMELIA HAD HAD all Mr. Thorncrest's orange trees moved into the ballroom, to his exceeding annoyance. The effect was exotic, much more so than that of the potted palms favoured by London hostesses, especially since several trees bore ripe fruit which glowed in the light of the chandeliers. Others were in bloom. Their fragrance wafted to meet Rowena as she made her curtsy to her hostess.

The party from Grove Park, arriving late at Millicent's behest, was immediately surrounded by young men. Most of the attention, as usual, clustered about the beauty, but several gentlemen previously unaware of Rowena's and Anne's existence requested dances with them.

"All because of my new dress," said Anne in disgust, though she did not refuse them. "My card is half full already. I must save some to sit out with Bernard. Do you see him, Rowena? Surely he has not already gone into the card room." She peered about the room.

Standing at an angle to the entrance, Rowena saw the earl and the captain bowing to Lady Amelia and Mr. Thorncrest. She told Anne, who swung round at once with her heart in her eyes. She would have rushed to greet them, or at least Captain Cartwright, but for Rowena's hand on her arm.

"Wait," said Rowena softly. "Hold yourself proudly, as Madame advised. He will come to you."

Lord Farleigh was still talking to his hostess when Bernard turned away from the receiving line. Anxious that her cousin should not expose her feelings to the tattlemongers, Rowena watched him. She saw his face light with wonder as he recognized Anne. His limp was scarcely visible as he came towards them, with eyes for none but her. He raised her hand to his lips and a faint colour rose in her cheeks. Not a word passed between them.

Consumed by envy, Rowena was taken by surprise when the earl spoke to her.

"You are out of mourning at last, Miss Caxton. How well green becomes you! One would think you a very wood nymph, especially in this orange grove." He was laughing, but there was admiration in his tone as well. "I hope you will celebrate your liberation by allowing me the honour of standing up with you."

"Thank you, my lord, that will be delightful." Rowena was pleased to note that her voice was composed. She offered him her dance card.

"I see I am not the only one to take advantage of your new freedom. If we had been delayed any longer I should have been too late. You are not engaged for the waltzes yet. Do you not waltz?"

"I have never danced it, but I have often watched and it does not look difficult. However, Millicent says that it is frowned on for a young lady to waltz without the permission of one of the patronesses of Almack's. Since I am unlikely to meet one, I ought not to do it."

"Fustian!" There was a wicked gleam in his grey eyes. "That rule is for *young* ladies, and you have admitted to attaining the ripe old age of one and twenty. I shall put my name down for two waltzes, Miss Caxton, and I'll not take no for an answer.''

"Yes, Major!" Not even the frowning presence of one of those patronesses could have stopped her.

He turned to ask Anne for a dance, and Rowena smiled sunnily at Millicent's scowl. It was not her fault the earl had spoken to her before approaching her cousin, and even Millicent had too much sense to make a scene at the ball. It was a pity that Lord Farleigh went straight from her side to Millie's, but it was inevitable. She was determined to enjoy the evening and not think about the future.

She looked at his signature on her card. It was a mirror of his character, firm, clear strokes leaving no room for ambiguity. And then, with a sense of shock, she realized two things: he had written not "Farleigh" but "Chris Scott"; and the second waltz was the supper dance.

That would surely set the cat among the pigeons!

She had no leisure to ponder either matter, for her first partner came to claim her hand. Mr. Desborough, son of Lord William, was one of those few who had always spared her a kind word, though in a stiffly condescending fashion she attributed to a sense of *noblesse oblige*. His manner had not changed, but he unbent sufficiently to compliment her on being in looks tonight. He was not one of Millicent's court, possibly because he scorned to compete. Rowena found him dull and a trifle pompous, but he was a good dancer and she loved to dance. She thoroughly enjoyed the cotillion.

After two more dances, she was quite happy to find a gap on her card before the first waltz with Lord Farleigh. She went to sit beside Anne, who was talking to Captain Cartwright. However, young Mr. Berry-

Browning came to remind Anne that she had promised to stand up with him for this dance, so Rowena was left with the captain.

They chatted for a while, then he fell silent, his gaze following Anne and her partner about the room. Rowena set her mind to the puzzle of the earl's signature.

The simplest explanation was that he was still unused to his title and had signed his name out of habit. In that case half the young ladies in the room might possess that signature, for his lordship was most conscientious about spreading his favours. She was not on sufficiently intimate terms with anyone but Anne and Millicent to ask to see their cards.

He might have meant to tease her with an allusion to her disregard for his rank. But surely he would have written "Major Scott," so that was not it.

She acknowledged a faint hope that he had signed his own name on her card only, and because when he was with her he thought of himself as plain Chris Scott, not as a peer of the realm. That would suggest that he was comfortable with her, more so than with his other partners. It was a pleasing notion, though she was sure he must have done it unintentionally. A deliberate gesture of that nature was foreign to his character.

She resolved to find a way to look at Anne's and Millicent's dance cards.

Then there was the business of his asking her for the supper dance. She sighed. He had probably not even noticed that it was anything more than a waltz, and if he had, he was undoubtedly unaware that it was a signal honour for a young lady to be chosen as his partner for supper. Millicent would be furious, though Mr. Ruddle had engaged her for that dance as soon as she entered the room.

"In a brown study, Miss Caxton? It is time for our waltz."

Startled for the second time that evening by his sudden appearance at her side, Rowena blinked up at Chris. His smile took her breath away.

She rose, and placed her fingertips on the arm he offered.

"I hope you were not worrying about your unfamiliarity with the steps?" he asked. "I have watched you dancing and I am sure so graceful a performer will have no difficulty."

He had watched her dancing! It was enough to render her speechless, but she refused to show so poor a spirit.

"No, my lord, that does not concern me. I have no doubt but that you will direct my steps, for I am familiar with your autocratic ways."

He grinned. "You malign me, ma'am. I've a mind to leave you to flounder without guidance."

"You are too much the gentleman, and besides, it would make you look as foolish as me."

"True, alas. Now start counting to the music, one two three, one two three." He swung her onto the floor.

"One two three, one two three," she repeated obediently, concentrating on following his lead.

The infectious rhythm caught her up, and she laughed with the exhilaration of the dance.

"We are not doing too badly for two self-confessed unmusical people," he observed as he twirled her round the room. "Now that I am sure you will not step on my feet, you may come a little closer." He pulled her towards him until only the few inches required by propriety separated them.

His hand holding hers, his strong arm about her waist, the warmth of his breath on her cheek—all should have flustered her. Instead she felt as if she belonged in his arms. Guided, protected, cared for—she was growing sentimental.

She summoned up mock indignation. "I have never stepped on a partner's feet."

"What, never? Perhaps wood nymphs are immune to such clumsiness. We soldiers, or rather our partners, are not so lucky. I waltzed for the first time at the Desboroughs' not a month since, and I fear Miss Desborough's toes must have been black and blue for days."

They continued to joke until the dance ended and he relinquished her to her next partner. With a deliberate effort Rowena forced herself to attend to Mr. Berry-Browning's trivial conversation as they took their place in the set for a country dance. Despite Lord Farleigh's distracting presence in the next set, of which she was constantly aware, she went through the figures of the Lancers without hesitation. The country hops and Canterbury assemblies of Kent had always been one of her favourite diversions.

When the time came for their second waltz Chris did not take her by surprise. Her consciousness of his whereabouts had continued though the length of the ballroom lay between them.

She heard herself laughing and chattering, yet she had no idea what she said. She must have answered appropriately, for he would not have failed to tease her if she had not, though he too seemed a trifle distrait. She was afraid the sight of Millicent waltzing with Mr. Ruddle was making him jealous.

However, when the blissful dance was over and they went into the supper room, he made no effort to join

Millicent's table. They sat with Anne and Bernard and Miss Desborough and her partner. Rowena was glad to see that Anne was no longer wearing her heart on her sleeve. Conversation was general and lively, and Miss Desborough's neighing laugh frequently rang out over the deeper voices of the gentlemen.

Rowena managed to catch a glimpse of both the other young ladies' dance cards. "Farleigh" was firmly inscribed on both.

As he held her chair when she rose from the table, Chris murmured, "I need your advice on fertilizing the cherry trees. I had almost forgot. You will not wish to rise early after dancing all night, so I will call tomorrow afternoon, if I may."

"Need you ask?" Rowena realized that not one word of agriculture had been spoken between them all evening. She need no longer tell herself he only sought her out for useful information.

After that exhilarating insight the rest of the ball could only be an anticlimax. Rowena was neither surprised nor disappointed when Millicent claimed a headache immediately after supper. Rowena had had her fling and not even her cousin's vapours or her aunt's admonishments had the power to spoil it.

"Indecorously coming behaviour, my foot!" said Anne vulgarly, sprawling on Rowena's bed in the small hours of the morning. "You had no need to cast out lures for they swarmed about you as soon as they saw your new gown. Is it not disgraceful the way pretty clothes make men change their opinion of you when inside you are the same person still? Not that it made the least difference to Bernard. He was the same as ever."

Rowena remembered the captain's dazzled expression when he first saw Anne in her new finery. She held her tongue. "All the same, it was pleasant to be noticed for once, was it not? I do love dancing."

"It was fun, but I had rather be riding. Bernard can ride. He has walked as much as two miles, too, but he is not ready to attempt to dance. He means to drive over tomorrow afternoon and try the walk back to the Grange." She yawned.

"Lord Farleigh is coming, too. He wants to know about fertilizing his cherries, but I don't know if I shall dare be so indiscreet as to discuss manure in your mama's parlour. Pinkie would have a spasm. You'd better go now or you'll fall asleep on my bed. Sweet dreams."

As soon as Anne shut the door behind her, Rowena slipped out of bed and went to the dresser. She rummaged in her reticule and withdrew two crumpled dance cards.

Her own she set down. The second was Millie's, picked up from the floor of the carriage.

She saw the signature at once: Farleigh. Tearing the card across she tossed the pieces on the embers smouldering in the grate. Picking up the other she traced the words with her fingertip. Chris Scott, and he had not discussed agriculture all evening.

That card went under her pillow.

A BANGING SHUTTER woke her about dawn. She felt for the card and went back to sleep, not to rouse again for several hours. A boisterous wind had risen during the night and violent gusts whipped the trees outside her window to a frenzy. The fire had gone out; a cold draught whistled down the chimney, stirring the ashes.

It was hard to persuade herself that she ought to get up, especially since Millicent, if she was awake, was no doubt drinking chocolate in bed. Still, Chris was coming this afternoon. By the time she had washed and dressed and eaten the enormous breakfast she felt in need of, he might be here. She rang for hot water.

The chambermaid was full of chatter about a tree that had blown down, breaking through the roof of a tenant's cottage. Sir Henry was already out seeing to emergency repairs.

"The master's a good landlord, miss, and her ladyship's right kind when there's trouble," the girl told Rowena.

Rowena would have liked to have been out there with her aunt, helping her to comfort the frightened family and making sure they had everything they needed. She shrugged. It was not her place to intervene. She was not likely ever again to have the pleasure of seeing those who relied on her content and wanting for nothing.

Her thoughts flew to Pinkie as she pulled on a warm woollen morning dress. Miss Pinkerton had been her chaperon and mentor, but she had been a dependent nevertheless. Now, despite her brave letters, it was obvious that she was leading a miserable existence bullied by her widowed sister-in-law. There was nothing Rowena could do about it. At least her tenants were not suffering, for according to Lady Farnhouse's occasional chatty communications, the new owner of Chillenden was a good master.

That did not bear thinking about. She picked up a shawl and went downstairs.

She had disposed of a plate of buttered eggs and ham and a couple of toasted muffins with marmalade before Anne joined her.

"What time do you think they will come?" Anne poured herself a cup of tea. "I'm not sure Bernard ought to go out in this wind. It's practically a hurricane."

"Not now. It has died down a great deal already. I daresay the captain is solid enough not to blow away. I always rather liked walking in windy weather. It's invigorating, especially when it is sunny like today. Not for riding, though. Perched on horseback you do feel exposed, as if any gust might carry you off." As she spoke, Millicent came in. "Good morning, cousin."

Millicent ignored the greeting and went straight to the attack. "What wiles did you use to persuade his lordship to take you in to supper?" she hissed at Rowena, taking up where she had left off the night before. "It is positively indecent the way you throw yourself at that man. You will be the laughingstock of the county."

Rowena had had more than enough, but she had no intention of falling into a vulgar squabble. Not deigning to reply, she pushed back her chair and rose. "Pray excuse me. I have finished my breakfast and I have some letters to be written."

As she left the room, back straight, chin high, she heard Anne plunging in with a comment guaranteed to lead to precisely the sort of undignified pulling of caps she deplored.

"It's you who will be the laughingstock for being so shrewish only because Rowena danced nearly every dance last night. *She* did not need any wiles to attract Lord Farleigh."

As Rowena made her way up to her chamber, she could almost find it in her heart to be sorry for Millicent. Brought up to consider her ability to attract men to be her only aim, she naturally lashed out when her preeminence in that regard was threatened. And because she had been taught that the worldly status of her husband was all important, she was liable to throw away the chance of happiness with the man she preferred for the dubious joy of being a countess.

Though Chris seemed dazzled by Millie's face and he needed her fortune, he was no fool. He would see through her charming façade sooner or later. And this very afternoon he was coming to Grove Park especially to see not Millicent but her. She danced up the last few steps.

Before going down to breakfast, she had given her prettiest new morning gown to Minton to be pressed. It was lying on her bed, a round dress of moss green Circassian cloth trimmed with peach-coloured ribbons and flounces. And there, in the middle of the bodice, was a flat-iron shaped scorch mark.

Minton appeared in the doorway. "I'm sure I'm sorry, miss," she said stiffly. "It was a banging shutter startled me. I can take a bit of the flounce from the back and cover it so it won't show hardly, but it'll take a while to do it proper."

Rowena knew the abigail had too much pride in her work ever to do such a thing deliberately. Besides, she was too happy to let such a little thing overset her.

"Please do that, Minton," she said cheerfully. "I shall wear something else this afternoon."

The village seamstress had so far delivered only one other suitable gown, of dark amber merino. Rowena took it from her wardrobe and hung it out to air. She trimmed her pen, but she was too restless to settle to her letters.

Though the gown was a rich colour that set off her hair nicely, it suddenly seemed too plain. If she had some écru lace to set in the décolletage in place of the ruffled muslin, it would only take Minton a few minutes to stitch it in. The village shop probably had something suitable, since she did not insist on Brussels lace. Ordinary Buckinghamshire was good enough for her.

She looked out of the window. Branches still tossed and fallen leaves swirled across the lawn, but the wind was playful now, not frenzied. A walk was just what she needed. Once again she went to the wardrobe and found an old walking dress.

"You must not let Millie drive you from the house, Rowena." Anne slipped into the room.

"Of course not." Rowena looked at her in surprise. She had forgotten all about Millie's megrims. "I told you I like to walk on a windy day. Besides, I mean to go down to the village and it is probably calmer down there. I suppose you do not care to come with me?"

Anne shook her head with an exaggerated shiver. "I mean to curl up in a rug with a book. Mama came in while Millie and I were at it hammer and tongs, and she has banished me to my room until dinnertime."

"But Bernard is coming to see you. Surely she will not be so unkind."

"I did not tell her. She would be bound to ask questions and I am not quite ready for that yet. Bernard will understand. There will be another day. Let me help you with those buttons if you *will* go, and you must wear a scarf under your hood or your hair will be shockingly tangled."

For a moment, Rowena was shaken by envy of Anne's faith in the captain.

The exhilaration of battling the wind soon restored her spirits. Walking briskly across the park, wrapped up warm in her cloak, she was glad she had decided not to ride Vixen. The gusts were stronger than she had thought, and some felt powerful enough to unseat anyone in a sidesaddle. Despite the scarf, strands of her hair blew free.

As she expected, once she reached the hedged lane it was calmer, and by the time she reached the stile she was warm enough to throw back the hood of her cloak. She even took off the scarf, though it was still breezy enough to make her wayward curls fly. In the orchard, blown leaves and twigs lay scattered on the ground, with a few larger branches. It crossed Rowena's mind that she might meet Chris riding out to inspect the damage to his trees. Some gentlemen might be shocked to see her with her hair in tangled knots; he would probably be amused. She loved the way his grey eyes glinted when he laughed.

She did not dawdle, though. He might well have gone in the opposite direction, and she wanted to be back at Grove Park when he arrived with his eager questions. Fertilizer was not precisely a romantic subject, but it was what he wanted to hear about and she was delighted to oblige.

In happy anticipation, she picked her way along the littered path.

CHAPTER THIRTEEN

"Do you think Sir Henry will be at home?" Bernard asked hopefully.

"Doubt it." Chris was filled with anticipation as he drove up the hill towards Grove Park. He was looking forward to seeing Rowena, and he could no longer pretend to himself that it was only for the benefit of her advice. He enjoyed her company.

"It's going to be ticklish discussing manure in Lady Grove's presence," he observed. "I wonder if I can somehow arrange to talk privately with Rowena without causing gossip, perhaps in the library with you and Anne to play chaperon?"

"I doubt Miss Grove will approve of that!"

He sighed. "No, and I cannot afford to vex her." It was a pity she was so easily offended. How it irked him that he needed her money. Neither her fortune nor her face could compensate for...

At that moment the curricle emerged from the shelter of the hedges and a gust of wind hit it broadside. His hat whirled away. It was all he could do to control his horses and retain his seat. A quick glance at Bernard showed him holding on for dear life with his good arm, clamping his beaver to his head with the other.

"Lord, the gale is blown up again! Are you all right?"

"Yes, but I'll walk home, I believe. Keep your eyes on your cattle!"

Chris nodded, obeying the injunction as another gust blasted out of nowhere. The horses strongly objected to the assault, while the light carriage rocked and swayed like a ship on the high seas. He hoped Bernard was not going to be seasick.

They reached the house before the captain had time to do more than turn a little green about the gills. Chris handed the reins to the groom who ran up.

"Stable them, if you please. I mean to ask if I may leave them here until the wind dies down."

"Right, my lord."

The gentlemen continued into the house and were ushered into the parlour. Millicent's golden curls were bent over an embroidery hoop. She looked up with an enchanting smile of welcome as they were announced.

"Oh, my lord, you startled me. How clumsy of me—I have pricked myself." She touched the tip of one delicate finger to her rosy lips, her blue eyes gazing into his own.

"Never clumsy, Miss Grove," he said gallantly. "I rue the day I caused you to hurt yourself. Allow me to bind up the injury." He reached for his pocket handkerchief, then remembered that he was carrying the one on which Rowena had embroidered his initial. For some reason he was reluctant to use it on Millicent's finger. "Bernard, have you a clean handkerchief?"

"Yes, I think so."

As Chris took his friend's place with Lady Grove by the roaring fire, he noted Millicent's pout. No doubt she would have preferred an earl to play doctor, he thought with unwonted cynicism. However, she then smiled prettily at Bernard and gave him her hand. Chris was ashamed of his suspicion.

He presented his compliments to her ladyship and begged leave to stable his horses at Grove Park overnight.

"Of course, my lord, and you and Captain Cartwright will be most welcome to spend the night here, too."

"You are very kind, ma'am, but we mean to walk home. The exercise will do us both good."

"To be sure, but I wish dear Rowena had not chosen to go out on such a very blustery day. I had to venture forth to see to the Perkinses—only think, a tree right through their roof in the middle of the night! It is a miracle that no one was hurt—but of course I had the carriage and my maid and the coachman with me."

"It is excessively odd in Rowena," agreed Millicent, joining them. "I fear she will be shockingly tousled when she comes in."

Chris frowned. He had told Miss Caxton he was going to call, that he had urgent need of her advice. He could think of no reason why she might wish to avoid him, unless he had inadvertently distressed her last night. He searched his memory, without success. They had had a delightful time together.

"Did Miss Anne go with Miss Caxton?" Bernard was enquiring.

"No, she is in her room. Perhaps I should send—"

Millicent interrupted her sadly indulgent parent. "Poor Anne is laid down with the headache," she said. "She is subject to megrims, you know. I daresay she strains her eyes with too much reading."

Bernard looked sceptical. Chris settled down to make the best of the visit, with some idea of awaiting Rowena's return. He could picture her bursting in with her honey-brown hair in disarray, her cheeks glowing from the exertion of battling the wind. She would look like a healthy, lively country girl, no match for Millicent's delicate beauty, but attractive in her own way. To him, much more—no, he durst not follow that train of thought.

The half hour proper to a visit was nearly passed when Lady Grove invited the gentlemen to partake of refreshments to fortify them against their walk home. The tea tray was sent for. It arrived with a full complement of scones and sweetmeats, including a plate of Banbury cakes. Since the earl had praised her cook's Banbury cakes, her ladyship had ordered them baked fresh daily, with plenty of currants, lest there should be an opportunity to offer them to him.

By the time tea had been poured by Millicent's graceful hand, and drunk, and the cakes consumed, twilight was falling. There was still plenty of time to walk home to the Grange, for Chris was sure that Bernard was strong enough, but he began to grow concerned about Rowena's prolonged absence.

"Is it not odd that Miss Caxton has not yet returned?" he suggested.

Lady Grove glanced worriedly at the window, then at the clock, and clasped her plump hands. "Oh, dear, yes. I am certain she did not mean to be gone so long. Whatever can have become of the child?"

"When did she go out?"

"I am not sure. One of the servants saw her leave. I have not seen her since breakfast."

"Since breakfast!"

"We breakfasted very late after the ball," Millicent pointed out. "And Rowena often takes lengthy walks."

"Have you any idea which way she went, ma'am?" Inside Chris, a hollow bubble of worry expanded. "Surely she mentioned to you where she was going, Miss Grove?"

"No, the silly creature tells me nothing."

"I daresay Miss Anne would know," Bernard suggested.

Anne was sent for at once. "She left right after breakfast," she announced. "I thought she had returned long since and was down here."

"Oh, dear, oh, dear, oh, dear, I did not realize she had been gone so long," wailed her ladyship.

"Did she say where she was going?" Chris demanded.

"Into Down Stanton, to make some purchase."

"I daresay she lingered to look about the shop," Millicent said airily, but even she appeared concerned.

"You can see everything in that shop in five minutes," Anne pointed out. "She has been gone for hours."

The bubble was threatening to choke Chris. "She would have taken the shortest way, I suppose." he managed to say.

"Yes," Anne was positive. "Down the lane then over the stile and through your orchards. Shall you look for her?"

"Yes, and we shall leave at once. Pray excuse us, ladies. Come, Bernard." Without another word Chris strode from the room, calling for his overcoat.

The wind had settled to a steady blow from the west, where gathering clouds hid the setting sun. It would have been possible to go home in the curricle, but Chris had no intention of deviating from the path Rowena had probably taken. Even driving down to the orchard gate they might miss her in the dusk. He set a brisk pace.

Bernard fell behind before they reached the park gates. Impatient, and angry with himself for his impatience, Chris waited. The girl had probably called on an acquaintance and forgotten the time, setting everyone by the ears for nothing.

"Go on without me," urged Bernard. "I could go faster but I don't want to be laid up for a week. Don't let me hold you back, Chris."

"It's ridiculous of me, but I have a dreadful feeling something has happened to her. She is such a reliable young woman in general, and she knew I was coming."

"Go on."

Chris strode ahead down the lane, his gaze searching the hedgerows, though what he expected to see he had no idea.

He waited again at the stile until Bernard came round the bend and within hailing distance.

"You know where the path to the village branches off from the path to the Grange," he called. "You go on home and I will carry on from there."

Bernard nodded and waved. He was walking at a steady pace, with only a hint of a limp. Chris vaulted the stile and went on.

It was gloomy between the unpruned trees and a couple of times he tripped over fallen branches strewn across the path. Bernard, going slower, should be able to avoid them. Perhaps Rowena had twisted her ankle and was hobbling painfully homeward. She would be surprised, delighted, to see him. He would pick her up and carry her to the gate, while Bernard sent the carriage to take her home. Or perhaps it would be better to

take her straight to the Grange for a reviving cup of tea
before . . .

A dark bulk sprawled on the path some fifty yards
ahead of him. He broke into a run, crashing through the
debris, his heart pounding.

Beneath a deadwood branch she lay on her side,
twisted, one forearm protecting her face. Her eyes were
closed and a jagged gash showed on her white temple.
Her hair was loose and full of bits of stick and leaves,
he noted irrelevantly.

"Bernard!" he roared as he exerted all his strength to
lift the heavy branch. "Bernard!"

The branch shifted, and now he moved with more
care lest some part of it strike her. At last she was free
and he dropped to his knees beside her, reaching for her
slender wrist as Bernard stumbled up to them.

"Her pulse is weak. I dare not carry her for fear of
doing more harm." Though he yearned to lift her slight
body in his arms, he had seen too many wounded men
crippled by being moved carelessly. "Can you make it
to the house? Send Potter and some others back with a
hurdle, and someone must ride for the doctor. Go as
quick as you can, Bernard."

"Of course." The captain hurried off, his limp more
pronounced now.

Chris ran his hands along Rowena's limbs, trying to
discover whether any bones were broken. It seemed not,
so with the utmost gentleness he straightened her
crumpled form. He took off his coat and spread it over
her. Powerless to help her further, he sat on the ground
beside her and picked a few scraps of bark out of her
tangled curls, then took her hand in his. It felt very
small and fragile.

He loved her. It was impossible to deny the overwhelming need for her that shook his body. If she would only open her eyes he would pour out his feelings, tell her she must live for his sake. Somehow his unready tongue would find the words to express all the sweet, confused emotions he had tried so long to avoid acknowledging.

She did not stir. It seemed forever he sat there in the deepening dusk holding her hand before he saw lanterns winking between the trees.

"Major, sir?"

"Potter! Over here. Thank heaven you've come."

"Quick as we could, sir. Bad, is she?"

"All I can find is a blow to the head, but there may be broken bones. Ned, Jemmy, set the hurdle here, close as you can, and hold the lanterns. Help me move her, Potter. Take her shoulders. Careful now."

"Easy does it, Major." The ex-corporal gently laid the unconscious girl on the hurdle then stooped, smoothing back her hair to look at the wound on her forehead. "A nasty bruise she'll have, but it's nought but a scratch. Bit of concussion, likely as not."

Rowena moaned and opened her eyes.

"Potter?" she murmured in puzzlement.

"Major, she's come round! Now don't you worry, miss, we'll have you home in a twinkling."

Chris instantly took his servant's place and bent over her. Her eyes were already closed, but a faint frown suggested that she had not swooned again.

"Rowena, I'm taking you to the Grange. You were hit on the head by a branch, and there may be other injuries. Keep as still as you can."

"Yes, Major," she whispered, the merest hint of a smile tugging at the corners of her lips.

She roused once more as the little procession made its way to the house. Chris saw the bewilderment in her green eyes as she glanced from one to another of the dark figures surrounding her. He held the lantern he carried so that the light fell on his face. Though she did not speak and he was not certain that she recognized him, the sight of him seemed to soothe her before she lapsed back into unconsciousness.

By the time they reached the Grange he was desperately worried about that prolonged insensibility. Diggory stood on the marble flight of steps to the front door, peering with unbutlerlike anxiety into the darkness. The two footmen flanking him ran down to relieve the grooms of their burden. They carried the hurdle into a vestibule that seemed unusually full of servants, who scurried out of sight as the butler reappeared.

"Mrs. Diggory has prepared the rose chamber for Miss Grove, my lord," he announced. "Oh, it is not Miss Grove. I understood it to be the young lady from Grove Park who sustained the injury."

"Miss Caxton," he snapped, realizing that she had never visited the Grange. "Carry her up, lads, and go carefully. Is the doctor sent for? Where is Captain Cartwright?"

Lady Farleigh answered him, limping out of the drawing room leaning heavily on her stick. "I sent Bernard to take a hot bath, Christopher, and then go to bed. He is not yet well enough to dash about the countryside on errands of mercy without suffering for it. The stableboy rode for the doctor, with a note from me to ensure his compliance."

"Thank you, ma'am. I must go up and make sure Miss Caxton is all right."

"You'll do nothing of the sort, young man. Mrs. Diggory and my dresser will manage very well between them. Lady Grove must be notified—Miss Caxton is her niece, I collect?—though I doubt the silly woman is of any use in a sickroom. When you have written and despatched an explanation to her, you may go and see Bernard."

"Yes, Lady F." Chris dropped a kiss on her smooth cheek as he passed. He had grown very fond of the dictatorial old lady, and her commands generally turned out to be common sense.

Though he itched to dash to Rowena's side, he realized that it was quite ineligible. He hurried to the library, scribbled a note to Lady Grove, and sent a footman to take it to the stables for a groom to bear up to Grove Park. There were advantages sometimes in having swarms of servants at his bidding.

He went up to see Bernard, who was already in bed, looking rather pale and wan.

"I ought to have left you with her and run back here myself," Chris said apologetically. "I was not thinking clearly."

"A shocking admission for a line officer. My leg aches like the very devil but you must not suppose there is anything serious the matter. How is Rowena?"

"Lady F. won't let me see her. Very proper, I suppose, but deuced frustrating. The doctor can look at your leg when he's seen to her."

"He need not, I only need to rest it."

"That's an order, Captain."

"Sir!" Bernard saluted mockingly.

"If only I had had those trees pruned of deadwood, this would never have happened."

"Don't tell me you are blaming yourself? You have been following Rowena's own instructions and you cannot suppose she will hold you responsible for her accident."

"No." Chris managed the ghost of a smile. "I expect she will tell me that even a major and an earl cannot command the winds." He paused as the door opened to admit Diggory, followed by a footman with a tray. "Ah, here is your dinner. Is it so late? I am still in all my dirt."

"I have had hot water carried to your chamber, my lord, but her ladyship asked me to inform you that she does not expect you to change for dinner." The butler looked down his long nose at Chris's nether garments, in which he had sat on the ground beside Rowena.

At least Jessup was no longer there to add his horrified disapproval. Chris washed his face and hands and went down to dinner as he was.

Halfway through the meal, a simple one as they had no guests, Chris heard the sounds of the doctor's arrival. Only Lady Farleigh's eagle eye prevented him from leaving the table to pace the hall outside Rowena's chamber. It seemed an age before he heard the man's footsteps descending the stairs.

"Diggory, ask Dr. Bidwell to join us here," ordered the dowager. "I daresay the poor man was interrupted at his dinner."

The doctor informed them, around a mouthful of apple tart, that Miss Caxton was suffering from a mild concussion, severe bruising and abrasions, and a slight fever as a result of exposure.

"Nothing to worry about, my lady," he added cheerfully. "I have left a draught to give her if she grows delirious. Someone should stay with her, but I do not expect any adverse developments. Send for me if she has not fully recovered her senses by noon tomorrow.''

"You may be sure we shall," said Chris grimly. He wanted to throttle the man for his blithe unconcern.

CHAPTER FOURTEEN

DR. BIDWELL HAS SCARCE DEPARTED when Anne arrived. She could be heard in the hall arguing with a footman. Before Chris could rise to his feet or Diggory had taken more than one step towards the dining room, she rushed in.

"Lord Farleigh, please tell your servant— Oh, my lady! I beg your pardon." She performed a hurried curtsy. "I am Anne Grove. I have come to take care of Rowena—my cousin."

"Alone, Miss Anne?"

Anne looked abashed. "It was useless even to ask Minton, ma'am. She's my sister's abigail. And with you and Rowena here... Our coachman brought me. You see, Mama did not wish to appear encroaching and Millicent pointed out that you have plenty of servants to look after Rowena."

"Peagoose!" snorted the dowager, but whether she referred to Lady Grove, Millicent, Minton or Anne was unclear.

Anne ignored the interruption. "I knew Rowena would be more comfortable with one of her family by her side. So I went to Papa and he said I might take the coach. Please say I may stay, ma'am?"

"Certainly." Her ladyship's tone was almost cordial. "Christopher, escort Miss Anne above stairs."

"Thank you, my lady." Anne curtsied again, then glanced about the room in alarm. "But where is Bernard? Is he hurt, too?"

Her eyes bright with interest, Lady Farleigh reassured her. "Nothing that rest will not cure. Dr. Bidwell tells us that *Captain Cartwright* merely overstrained weak muscles running for help."

Anne flushed at the pointed use of Bernard's rank and surname.

"I shall tell you all about it." Chris came to her rescue, taking her arm and leading her from the room.

He delivered her to the rose bedchamber, where he was firmly denied entrance by Mrs. Diggory. Disconsolate, he wandered back to Bernard's room and told him of Anne's arrival and *faux pas*.

"What a dear she is," the captain murmured drowsily. The doctor had left a sleeping draught to ease his pain.

Chris went down to the drawing room and drove Lady Farleigh to distraction with his pacing. It was there that Mrs. Diggory found him an hour or so later. A motherly woman quite unlike her imposing husband and imperious mistress, the housekeeper had had little to do with her new master. She was astonished when he approached her eagerly and seized both her hands.

"How is she?"

"Miss Caxton's still out to the world, my lord." She tried to curtsy and he released her. "Her forrid's a bit hot, but she's lying peaceful enough. Miss Anne wants to sit up with her. Will that be all right, my lady?"

"I daresay, but see that a maid stays with them." She sounded querulous. "Christopher, help me up the stair, I shall retire now. All these alarums and excursions are too much for me at my age."

Chris decided he might as well go to bed, too. Perhaps in the morning he might be allowed to see Rowena.

The old habit of sleeping lightly lest Bernard should call out came back to him. He half-roused several times, heard nothing and went back to sleep. Then came a muffled cry that brought him instantly to full alertness. He flung his dressing gown on over his nightshirt and hurried into the hallway, tying the girdle as he went.

There it was again, clearer now, from the rose bedchamber. Without ceremony he opened the door and went in.

By the flickering light of the fire and a pair of candles on the mantel, he saw Rowena tossing restlessly on the bed. Her eyes were open but unfocussed. Anne bent over her, trying to calm her. She looked up as he strode to her side.

"I cannot keep her still, let alone give her the doctor's draught."

"Where is the maid Lady Farleigh bade stay with you?"

Anne waved at a dark corner. "She is so sound asleep that Rowena's cries did not disturb her, and I did not dare leave Rowena to go and shake her."

The cry came again. "Pinkie, my head hurts so. Pinkie? Don't go away again."

Chris sat on the edge of the bed, put his arm round Rowena's shoulders and captured her agitated hands in his.

"Rowena, be still and take your medicine."

She froze, then her eyes cleared a little and she mumbled, "Yes, Major."

Anne hastened to raise the cup to her lips and she obediently swallowed. Then she let Chris ease her down on the pillows and Anne pulled up the coverlet and tucked her in firmly.

"Will you stay with me, Pinkie?" Her eyes were closing already.

"I shall stay," Anne promised.

"And I," Chris added softly. They sat in silence until her even breathing told them she was asleep, then he said in a low voice, "Who is Pinkie?"

"Her cousin, Miss Pinkerton. Rowena keeps calling for her."

"Would she come, do you think, if I sent my carriage to fetch her?"

Anne stared at him. "Would you do that? I expect she will for they are very fond of each other, and she is not happy where she is, I collect. It always troubled Rowena that she could do nothing for her."

"You do not know her direction, I suppose."

"I have often seen Rowena's letters to her lying on the hall table." A moment's thought produced an address in Islington.

"I'll send Potter first thing in the morning. Bernard was right when he said that your intellect is superb." He was teasing, for remembering an address was hardly a test of intellect.

"He said that?" The dim light could not hide her pink cheeks and the way her eyes sparkled. "That is the nicest compliment I have ever had. And all the better that he did not say it to my face."

"You are an unusual girl, Miss Anne." Chris grinned and shook his head. "Nonetheless, you must be tired and I have had a few hours' sleep. Might I suggest that you lie down on the chaise by the fire? I will watch your cousin and I promise to wake you if her condition changes. I am quite an expert nurse, I assure you."

"Of course, you have had a great deal of practice. I...I hope you will not think me forward if I thank you for taking care of Bernard?"

"Not at all," he said gravely.

She settled on the chaise longue and soon drifted off to sleep. He saw her pelisse draped over the back of a chair and spread it over her, then stood a moment looking down at her. He envied his friend. There was nothing to stop Bernard offering for Anne, and everything to stop Chris offering for Rowena. Beautiful as Millicent was, he did not love her, and he knew very well that she did not love him, yet for her money's sake he must woo her. It made him feel a villain.

Rowena moaned and he hurried to her. Despite Bernard's reassurances he still blamed himself at least in part for her mishap. She looked frail and lost in the middle of the wide bed.

He suddenly remembered the young man who had sent her horse to her; perhaps she would want him informed of her illness. Jealousy flared as he wondered just how close Rowena had been to her old neighbour. Nonetheless, if she wished to see the fellow he would do his best in the morning to contact him.

For now, though, all he could do was to make her as comfortable as possible. Anne, in a laudable attempt to keep her still, had tucked in the bedclothes so tight that they must be pressing painfully on her bruises. Chris loosened one side. As he leaned over to tug at the other, she moved in her sleep, pushing down sheet and coverlet. His hand brushed her breast, clad only in a thin cotton bedgown.

He started back as if he had been burned. An unaccustomed warmth spread through him. Lady Farleigh was probably right, he should not be here.

He stayed. He found some lavender water and bathed her hot forehead, avoiding the small piece of court plaster. He murmured soothing words when she stirred and held her hand when she moaned, and when, towards dawn, she opened her eyes, his face was the first thing she saw.

"Chris." Her smile wavered.

"Thank heaven, you have regained your senses. How do you feel?"

"My head feels as if a blacksmith is at work inside."

"My poor girl!"

"What happened? Where am I?" Rowena's voice was scarcely audible and she had closed her eyes again.

"You are at Farleigh Grange. Do you remember walking... Oh, Lord, the maid is stirring and I ought not to be here. Call to her if you need anything, and your cousin Anne is asleep by the fire, too. I shall come and see you later, I promise, and explain everything." He quickly pressed her hand and slipped out of the room.

There was a small desk in his dressing room, an exquisite piece of French buhl that had probably cost enough to pay a dozen day-labourers for a year. Chris sat down and struggled with the composition of a letter that without unduly alarming the elderly spinster, would bring Miss Pinkerton racing to her young kinswoman's side.

By the time it was done to his satisfaction, he heard servants moving about. The door swung open to admit a chambermaid bearing a coal-scuttle. When she saw him sitting there in his dressing gown she gasped, set the scuttle down with a thump on the carpet and bobbed a curtsy.

"Beg pardon, my lord. I di'n't know your lordship were awake. I c'n come back later."

"Never mind the fire, just go and tell Potter I need him, if you please."

"Yes, my lord." Again she curtsied, then turned and fled. He heard whispering and giggling in the hall and wondered how many chambermaids he employed.

"Go and ask Mrs. Diggory," one voice advised, and there was a pattering of feet.

Noting with annoyance the dirty mark left on the priceless Aubusson carpet, Chris picked up the scuttle and made up the fire. He had often done it in Spain, after all, and the room was chilly.

It was ten minutes before Potter arrived, dressed with somewhat less than his usual military neatness.

"I thought we was done with reveille at dawn, my lord," he said with disapproval. "Them maids is in a right flutter what with you being up at this hour and telling 'em to wake his lordship's own personal vally de chamber. That's like sending a raw recruit to wake a drill sergeant, that is."

"Enough of your lip, corporal. I've marching orders for you."

"Sir!" Potter sprang to attention.

Chris gave him the letter for Miss Pinkerton. "You'll take the travelling carriage. It's up to you to make sure the old lady is comfortable, but see that you get her here by tomorrow night. Miss Caxton wants to see her."

"Not like to stick her spoon in the wall, is she, my lord?"

"No, but she is far from well."

"Poor lass. By all accounts she's well liked up at Grove Park."

"That's enough, corporal! Let's have a little discipline around here, even if I'm no longer an officer, merely an earl."

Potter grinned, but said only, "Yes, sir." He saluted and departed.

Chris wanted to go back and see if Rowena was still awake. Failing that, he wandered over to the window. His rooms were at the front of the house, and the carriage would pass on its way to the main gate. Rowena had called for Pinkie, and Pinkie she should have. If his situation denied him the happiness of making her his wife, at least he should have the satisfaction of fulfilling her least wish.

The limetrees lining the avenue were still now, but the ground beneath them was littered with branches. The Earl of Farleigh sighed. He had better dress and go to see what damage the tempest had wrought in his precious orchards.

Most of the few remaining apples had been blown off the trees. They were unsalable, fit only for immediate use. He decided to open the orchards to gleaners; that would please Rowena. Several trees had blown down, but they were all among those he meant to replace anyway. He shuddered at the thought that Rowena might have been hit by a tree instead of just a branch.

The wind had done quite a bit of his pruning for him, as well as stripping most of the leaves from the branches. He must ask Rowena whether the pruning could proceed at once, or whether he must wait another month or two for the trees to become truly dormant.

He hoped she would be well enough to consult. He must be careful not to tire her with his questions.

It was still early when he returned from his ride, but his bailiff and two of his tenants were waiting for him. Tentatively at first, then with more confidence when they realized his lordship was not about to send them off with a flea in the ear, they presented their damage reports.

A henhouse had been demolished and a chimney toppled, besides an astonishing number of slates off the roofs. Mr. Deakins had already worked up an estimate of the cost of repairs.

Though Chris blenched when he saw the total, he nodded. "I'll dub up, but I want to see for myself first. Shall we go, gentlemen?"

It was more essential than ever that he marry a fortune. He simply could not allow himself to see Rowena as anything more than a friend.

El Cid was saddled again and Chris rode round all the farms with Mr. Deakins. None of the others had suffered quite as much, fortunately for his pocket. He ordered his bailiff to set repairs in train and once more returned home anxious to consult Rowena, if she felt well enough. He had not the least notion whether the prices quoted were reasonable, but she would surely know.

As he approached the vestibule from the stable entrance he heard the front door opening. He was disinclined to receive visitors, especially when he heard Millicent speaking.

"We have come to see my cousin, Miss Caxton."

Diggory replied in his dignified tones, "I shall send to inform Miss Caxton of your arrival, my lady, miss. Her ladyship is in the drawing room; will you wait there?"

"The earl is not at home?" There was an unmistakable pout in Millicent's voice.

Chris braced himself to do his duty. "I have just now returned, ladies." He bowed.

"Oh, there you are, Lord Farleigh. We are come to make sure poor Rowena is all right."

"Of course you must be concerned," he said, trying to keep the irony out of his voice as he thought of their notable absence last night. "I have not heard the latest news, but if you will come into the drawing room Diggory will soon bring us word."

Lady Grove protested her gratitude at his rescue of her niece, and repeated fulsome thanks to Lady Farleigh for taking Rowena in.

"Of course we will take her home with us at once if she is well enough," she added. "The poor child will do better in her own home."

"Oh, no, Mama, we must not think of moving Rowena until she is quite recovered," Millicent insisted. "How selfish it would be to risk her health because we want her at home! I am sure Lady Farleigh's servants are well able to care for her."

"Not to mention your sister, who hurried to her side last night," said the dowager sardonically.

"Anne is the veriest hoyden, I fear, ma'am." As usual Lady Grove was easily flustered. "It would not occur to her that her presence might discommode the household."

"On the contrary, ma'am, I found her solicitude admirable."

To Chris's relief, Anne came in at that moment.

"Mama, I am so glad you are come. Rowena's poor head aches so. I do not know what to do for her." Belatedly she curtsied to the countess. "Good morning, my lady. Pray excuse us?"

"Go on, child, be off with you," Lady Farleigh waved dismissal.

Chris accompanied Anne and her mother to the door. "Is she feverish again?" he asked. "No? Well, I shall send for Dr. Bidwell again, anyway." He gave orders to that effect, then returned to the drawing room to speak to the dowager. Only then did he realize that Millicent had stayed behind.

"Do you not wish to see your cousin?" He frowned.

"It cannot be good for Rowena to receive a crowd. Much as I long to see her, I must not jeopardize her recovery. Do you dine at the Berry-Brownings' tomorrow, my lord?"

He listened impatiently to her chatter about the social engagements already scheduled for the next week or two. It disgusted him that she was more interested in such matters than in her cousin's health, and he began to wonder whether he could really bear to marry her. He felt Lady Farleigh's satirical gaze on him. Millicent seemed to become aware of her unreceptive audience and changed the subject, talking admiringly of the magnificence of the Grange.

"I quite long to dance in your splendid ballroom, sir," she cooed. "Do say that you mean to hold a ball soon, or perhaps a masquerade. Yes, a masquerade would be prodigious amusing, would it not?"

"I cannot plan entertainments while I have two sick guests in the house."

"Oh, no, when they are well again. Two? Who is the other?"

"Captain Cartwright has received a setback. In fact, I have not seen him this morning. You will excuse me, ladies, if I go up to him now."

"Of course, Christopher. Ask dear Bernard if the embrocation I sent has helped at all. Miss Grove and I shall have a comfortable cose."

Millicent looked appalled but did not dare protest.

Bernard was sitting up on his bed, reading a book propped at a convenient angle by a pile of pillows.

"Is Anne still here?" he asked eagerly as Chris entered his chamber. "Do you suppose she might be allowed to visit me? Incapacitated as I am, I cannot surely be considered a threat to her virtue."

"I'll see what I can do. Properly chaperoned, of course! Her mother and sister are here, too. Lady Grove and Anne are with Rowena. I feel somewhat guilty at leaving the fair Millicent to Lady F.'s tender mercies, but she will rattle on about parties—to hide her concern, I daresay." He tried to convince himself.

"I daresay."

"It was considerate of her to choose not to tire Rowena with too many visitors."

"Most considerate."

"Oh, go to the devil. I know she is no angel. I fear she regards Rowena's accident as a convenient excuse for calling here often."

"Be careful, my lad, you are growing quite puffed up."

"Never!" said Chris in horror. He hastened to explain, "I am all too well aware it is my rank she covets, not my person. But enough of the chit. Lady F. wants to know if her embrocation has helped your leg."

"In order to be allowed below stairs to see Anne, I will say it has cured me completely."

"But you are still in considerable pain, are you not? Don't worry, I shall smuggle her in here if I have to. *She* is not like to have any objection."

"Do you think not?" Bernard asked eagerly.

"I am prepared to wager my estate on it. Not that it would be any great loss." He described the havoc wrought by the gale. It was a relief to talk about it, even though his friend had no words of wisdom to offer.

When he left the room, Lady Grove and Anne were just leaving Rowena's chamber. Lady Grove looked distraught.

"Oh, my lord," she cried on seeing him, "the poor child is most unwell. I do not know what is best to do for her. I was never easy in a sickroom, I fear. She has taken the doctor's draught however, so I daresay she will feel more the thing presently."

"Please say I may stay, sir," Anne begged. "Mama says I must not trespass upon your hospitality, but Rowena needs me."

"If Lady Grove will be good enough to give her permission, Miss Anne, I hope you will stay, at least until Miss Pinkerton comes. Perhaps I ought to have consulted you, ma'am, but I took the liberty of sending for Miss Caxton's old companion."

"That was monstrous kind in you, I vow."

"But she will not be here until tomorrow, Mama. Say I may stay, please."

Beset on all sides, Lady Grove conceded.

CHAPTER FIFTEEN

"I JUST WANT TO SEE if there is anything I can do to make you more comfortable. Your aunt says you are not at all well," Chris said anxiously.

"I took Dr. Bidwell's draught, and now I feel much better. Before that I ached all over, much worse than when I rode Vixen that day." Unexpectedly Rowena giggled. Her eyes seemed very green, despite the dim room, its crimson brocade curtains drawn against the glare of daylight.

The thought of her suffering troubled Chris, with an almost physical malaise. "You will be black and blue for some days, I collect." He tried to reassure her. "The doctor swears the headache will pass."

"At least it is gone for now, sir. I feel like talking. Did the wind do much damage in the orchards, besides the branch that hit me?"

Chris accepted this invitation with alacrity and poured out his questions, forgetting Mrs. Diggory who was on duty in the sickroom. Rowena responded eagerly, almost impatiently, scarcely waiting for him to finish a phrase. At last Chris noticed the housekeeper peering in an ostentatious way at the watch pinned to her starched black bodice.

"Fifteen minutes, my lord, and not a moment longer, that's what her ladyship said."

"Never fear, Mrs. Diggory, I do not dare cross her ladyship. Thank you, Miss Caxton, as always you have given me everything I need. I will not trespass further on your generosity, for I know you ought to be resting. Just tell me one thing: do you want me to inform Geoffrey—I forget the last name—about your accident?"

"Geoffrey? Geoff Farnhouse? Why on earth should I want you to write to Geoff?"

"I thought, since he sent you your horse, that there must be some sort of understanding between you."

"We were practically brother and sister. Oh, he did want to marry me when our estates marched together, but we were never anything to each other except good friends."

Chris felt as if a constricting neckcloth had been removed from his throat. It was the oddest sensation.

"Anne said you have sent for Pinkie." Rowena smiled drowsily, suddenly on the brink of sleep. "That is quite the kindest thing you could have done."

"I have tired you," he said in self-reproach, touching her hand lightly. "Go to sleep now." He tiptoed from the room.

"Yes, dear Major," she whispered to his departing back.

"Well, I never, to think of his lordship's asking your advice like that, miss. There's many round here'll be that grateful if you put him in the way of straightening things out." Mrs. Diggory felt her forehead. "No fever still, thank the Lord, but before you settle, try if you can to drink a drop of this nice barley water Cook made up for you, my dear."

When Anne came in to take her turn at the bedside, Rowena awakened with a return of the splitting headache. Full of the brief visit to Bernard Lady Farleigh had allowed, Anne chattered without requiring a response while she spooned a sustaining broth into Rowena's mouth. She was dubious about giving another dose of the doctor's draught so soon, but Rowena's head was so bad that she relented. It tasted horridly bitter, but as before the aches vanished and after a brief period of restlessness she fell asleep again.

When she awoke the next morning her head hurt worse than ever though her bruises were much less painful. She bore with what complaisance she could muster a visit from Aunt Hermione, who fussed unbearably and insisted on shaking up the pillows twice in twenty minutes. However, she refused to take any more medicine. Even without it, as the day passed her headache faded, and when Chris came in, late in the afternoon, she looked forward to a long discussion.

"I won't stay more than five minutes," he said at once. "I had a rare trimming yesterday from Lady F. for tiring you. Mrs. Diggory is a tale bearer, I fear." He grinned at the indignant housekeeper.

"Nowt of the sort, my lord! I'd like to know how I'm to answer a straight question from her ladyship if not with the truth. You've four minutes left."

"And a regular martinet. You look a little better today, Miss Caxton, so I cannot think my visit was so damaging to your health."

"Oh, no, indeed it was not. I should be sadly dull if I had not something to think of. Tell me how things are going with the tenants' repairs."

He gave her a quick progress report.

"Time's up, my lord," announced Mrs. Diggory, consulting her watch.

"Yes'm." Chris stood up and smiled down at the invalid. "I have every hope that your Miss Pinkerton will be here this evening, Rowena. Potter had orders to hurry back."

"No doubt he will scarce stop to change the horses, then. Poor Pinkie, but how I long to see her!"

She watched him leave with his firm, soldierly stride, his upright military bearing. That was the second time he had called her Rowena. It was a slip of the tongue, of course, yet surely it must mean he thought of her as a friend, not only a mentor. And he had come to see her, even though he had no questions for her. She almost hoped the headaches would continue so that she could stay at the Grange indefinitely.

Content, she let her gaze wander about the room. Though it had nothing to do with her desire to remain, she was duly impressed by the magnificence of her chamber. The walls were hung with rose silk; ornate plasterwork in a fanciful design of climbing roses and cupids decorated the ceiling; and the mantel was of pink-veined marble. No wonder there had not been a penny to spare for the land, she thought indignantly.

Her next visitor limped into the room, cane tapping, just before the dinner hour. Lady Farleigh, eyes bright with curiosity, studied Rowena with embarrassing intentness as she crossed the room and sat down beside the bed.

"So you are the young woman who caused all the to-do. We have not met."

"No, ma'am. You must be Lady Farleigh. Thank you for your hospitality, my lady. It is excessively kind in you to allow me to stay."

"Gammon! I had no say in the matter—it was all young Christopher's doing. And then the boy pestered me to let him see you."

Rowena was annoyed to feel a flush rising in her cheeks under the old lady's scrutiny. "I have been telling... His lordship has done me the honour of seeking my advice on running his estate, ma'am. I have some experience with a similar place in Kent."

"So I hear. Most commendable."

"Lord Farleigh just wanted to consult me on some urgent matters."

"Ah, that would account for it." The dowager countess looked as if she did not credit Rowena's explanation for a moment. "It is odd that your aunt never brought you to the Grange."

"I...I am in some sort a companion to my cousin Millicent, my lady. I daresay Aunt Hermione thought it unnecessary for me to pay my respects."

"And now the beauteous Miss Grove does not deign to visit her cousin and companion. She was here again this morning, ready to throw her cap over the windmill at the slightest sign from Christopher. She'll catch cold at that game if I have anything to say in the matter, for all her splendid dowry. And her sister no better—young ladies did not ask to visit gentlemen in their bedchambers in my young day, I declare!"

"Oh, no, ma'am, the case is quite different. Anne and Captain Cartwright are truly in love."

"Hmm, that's the impression Christopher gave me, or I should not for a minute have countenanced such indecorum. And only his need of your advice persuaded me to permit him to see you. Well, enough on that head." She struggled to her feet. "I'll not tire you further. Just remember, Miss Caxton, that there are times when knowledge is worth more than any fortune."

She hobbled out, leaving Rowena to ponder the significance of her last remark. It sounded astonishingly as if the dowager would approve a match between the earl and the poor relation.

MISS PINKERTON ARRIVED while Rowena was eating her dinner. She had graduated from broth to minced chicken and a custard, and Anne no longer had to help her. She abandoned her tray with a glad cry when Pinkie scurried in, breathless with excitement.

"My love, how good it is to see you."

"Oh, Pinkie, I have missed you!" Rowena hugged her.

"So very kind of Lord Farleigh... Such a comfortable carriage... And Lady Farleigh received me most graciously. How are you, Rowena dear? What a shocking accident!"

"Still a trifle out of curl, but much better for seeing you."

"Rowena is much improved, ma'am," Anne interposed, curtsying, "but we are worried about her headaches. She received a shocking blow to the head, you know."

"Yes, indeed, Corporal Potter told me. Rowena, where are your manners? Pray introduce us."

"My cousin Anne Grove, Pinkie, and she knows very well who you are, for she conspired with his lordship to send for you. You must not worry about my head. It is much better tonight and I still have some of the doctor's draught to help me sleep."

"And it is time you took it and went to sleep, if you do not mean to eat any more," said Anne, demonstrating her newfound nursing skills.

"Oh, dear, I might have guessed. Is that the draught, Miss Anne? May I see it?" Miss Pinkerton uncorked the brown bottle, raised it to her nose and sniffed, then poured a drop of the contents on her finger. She tasted it with the tip of her tongue. "Laudanum!" she said triumphantly. "Rowena never could take laudanum. First she grows agitated, and then afterwards there is always the dreadful headache. I'll just pop down to the kitchens and see if the cook can brew up some chamomile tea."

"I'll go. You must be tired after the journey, Miss Pinkerton. Chamomile tea, you said?"

"That's what she needs, mark my words." Pinkie beamed and nodded as Anne hurried out. "A pretty-behaved young woman," she said to Rowena, "though I will say I was predisposed by your letters to like her. Now, my dear, you lie quietly till she comes back and I will stay with you until you fall asleep. We shall talk tomorrow."

Holding Pinkie's hand, Rowena lay back against the pillows and closed her eyes. She had not realized how much she missed being important to someone close to her. Anne was a dear and a good friend, but for some time now she had been absorbed in her feelings for the captain. Pinkie was hers, and hers alone.

The chamomile tea was soothing, besides tasting much better than the medicine. Rowena slept soundly and awoke with no more than a slight tenderness where the branch had hit her head. Her chief ailment now was weakness from lying so long abed, so Pinkie insisted that she leave it to recline on the chaise by the fire for half an hour.

She was there when Chris came in to see her. The half hour stretched to an hour, and then to an hour and a half as they talked, first about the orchards and tenants, then moving on to a hundred other subjects. Miss Pinkerton watched and listened indulgently. She had had a long interview with Lady Farleigh that morning. The two elderly ladies found themselves in accord on any number of matters, from the disgraceful informality of modern manners to an elegant menu for an October dinner party. There was just enough of disagreement left (Miss Pinkerton could not, for instance, allow the superiority of the Bodley over the Yorkshire kitchen range) to promise hours of agreeable discussion.

By the time she saw that Rowena was tiring and chased his lordship out, she was convinced that the countess was right on two counts that she had doubted.

She helped her charge's wobbly steps back to the bed and tucked her in.

"I believe you will be ready to go below stairs for a while tomorrow," she said.

"I must not recover too soon, or I will lose you again." Rowena looked at her anxiously. "Though perhaps my aunt will invite you to stay for a little while."

Pinkie made her next announcement with the air of a whist player producing the ace of trumps. "Lady Farleigh has asked me to stay with her indefinitely."

"But she only met you for the first time yesterday!"

"Her ladyship prides herself on being a quick judge of character, I collect. She took a liking to you yesterday, my dear, and was so kind as to congratulate me on whatever small part I had in forming your disposition. She says she would like me to be her companion when she removes to the Dower House, which she expects to be soon."

"She . . . she does?"

"To be sure. Now no more chatter or you will not go down tomorrow after all."

Rowena lay quietly but could not sleep. There was too much to think about. Lady Farleigh obviously expected Chris to marry soon, but there was no knowing who would be the lucky bride. The dowager seemed to dislike Millicent, yet Chris would make up his own mind, and his strong sense of responsibility to his tenants must encourage him towards marrying a fortune. Rowena had to admire his loyalty, though it worked against her. She would not love him so much if he was ready to abandon his dependents to follow his own inclination.

She was beginning to dare to hope that his inclination was turning towards her. He had stayed so long this afternoon, and after the first few minutes they had scarcely mentioned agriculture. He had talked about his early childhood in Dorset, his youth in London, his sister, married to a Dorset squire with a brood of children he knew only from brief visits on leave from the war.

Rather than following his father in the law, he had joined the army at nineteen. Rowena imagined him, proud and excited in his first uniform, and wished she had known him then, before the horrors of battle had set their stamp on his stern countenance. She loved the way his eyes softened when he talked of his nephews and nieces. He ought to have a brood of children of his own, and she wanted desperately to be their mother.

And yet, as his adviser, she could not in all honesty recommend that he choose herself as his wife.

If he married Millicent, at least her cousin would be gone from Grove Park, and Pinkie would be living nearby. Rowena tried to persuade herself that that was consolation enough.

CHAPTER SIXTEEN

AN INEXPLICABLE NERVOUSNESS made Chris's knock tentative as he stood before the door of Rowena's chamber.

"Who is it?" called Miss Pinkerton.

"Chris...that is, it's Farleigh, ma'am. Lady Farleigh sent me to help Miss Caxton down the stair."

"Just a minute."

He waited, shifting from one foot to the other, until the door opened.

"Come in, my lord. She is ready."

His gaze flew to Rowena. She was sitting on the bedside chair, dressed in an amber gown trimmed with lace, her golden brown curls tumbling about her shoulders. Her face was pale, tired from the effort of dressing, but all he saw was the smile of welcome on her lips and in her green eyes. His uncertainty fled as he smiled back.

"Will you allow me to carry you down, Miss Caxton? Lady F. roundly damned me for thinking to entrust so precious a burden to a footman."

Rowena's eyes widened, and Miss Pinkerton looked at him with approval and no small degree of satisfaction.

"Very proper, my lord," she said blandly.

Rowena was speechless but as he went about the clumsy business of picking her up, one arm round her shoulders, the other beneath her knees, she giggled.

"I was half afraid you meant to sling me over your back. This is much more comfortable, but I fear it is awkward for you."

"It will be easier for his lordship to carry you if you put your arms about his neck," Miss Pinkerton instructed.

Chris saw the colour rise in her cheeks and she made no move to comply.

"Please do, Rowena," he said softly. "Miss Pinkerton is right, it will help."

He was unprepared for the tide of feeling that rushed through him at the soft touch of her hands on the back of his neck. Shaken, he held her closer and turned to stride out of the room, bearing a burden that was suddenly very precious indeed. The emerald eyes, so close to his, were veiled with long lashes. He wanted to kiss the rosy lips, slightly parted as if she were breathless, too. He felt the rapid beating of her heart and wondered if she felt his, if she could sense the emotion coursing through him. How could he have been so blind all that time as to think of her only as his counsellor and friend!

All too soon they reached the hall and Diggory was swinging open the door of the drawing room. Rowena's gaze met Chris's. Whatever she saw in the eyes she claimed to read so easily, she gave a tiny gasp and her slender arms tightened briefly about his neck.

"On the sofa by the fire, Christopher." Lady Farleigh's command broke the moment.

With the utmost gentleness he set her down on the couch. Only the presence of the dowager, Miss Pinkerton and Bernard stopped him running his fingers down her cheek and asking if there was any hope . . .

"Miss Grove, Mr. Ruddle," announced Diggory.

Millicent glided in, beautiful as ever in celestial blue, her escort following dressed in mauve. After one glance and a slight bow, Chris returned his gaze to Rowena's bent head. As he leaned over her to ask if she needed a glass of wine to revive her, he was vaguely aware of Millicent's prattling about Mr. Ruddle's kindness in bringing her to see how her cousin did.

"No...yes...thank you, I..." Rowena stammered, raising her eyes as far as his neckcloth.

He took her hand and pressed it. "Better have something. You will need to fortify yourself to face our visitors, and Anne and your aunt are not far behind, I daresay."

As he poured a glass of canary, he looked back at Rowena. She was holding the hand he had touched to her cheek. His aim wavered and he spilled several drops of the wine.

He was behaving like a callow youth in the first throes of calf love. With a deliberate effort he steadied himself and returned to her, setting the glass on a table at her elbow and pulling up a chair close by. He became aware that Bernard was regarding him with a knowing grin, while Millicent pointedly ignored him.

"I am glad you are so much better, Rowena," she said sweetly. "You will be able to drive home with Mama and Anne, I expect."

Lady Farleigh and Miss Pinkerton both hastened to assure her that it was out of the question for several days yet. However, Millicent's knowing smile made Chris's heart sink.

"You are prodigious kind, ma'am, but I am sure Mama will not permit Rowena to discommode you any longer."

As he had predicted, Lady Grove and her younger daughter arrived a few minutes later. The merest suggestion from Millicent convinced her mother that in view of Rowena's rapid recovery, the inconvenience of her stay at the Grange must come to an end. Even Lady Farleigh was unable to persuade her, under Millicent's minatory eye, to extend the convalescent's visit by more than a day.

Millicent retired triumphant to flirt with Mr. Ruddle. Chris turned his back on her.

"Your cousin is quite wrong, you know," he assured Rowena with quiet fervour. "Your presence is not an inconvenience but a delight—to all of us. I must not gainsay your aunt, of course, but I cannot think the journey will be good for you."

"I shall be sorry to go." Her soft voice was unwontedly shy, and she met his gaze uncertainly. "But it is scarce any distance."

"True." He could ride to Grove Park in less than a quarter of an hour, and surely even Millicent could not hide her from him. "If go you must, you shall go in my carriage, with every pillow and cushion I possess to soften the way for you."

She laughed. "On the seats, or under the wheels? I daresay there are enough in the house to pave the lane all the way up the hill."

"Would that I could! But the carriage is well sprung. My predecessor did occasionally spend a little blunt on something other than bricks and mortar."

She reached out and touched his hand. "Don't be bitter, Chris. It can only hurt you."

"Don't you ever resent your father's lack of care for your future? No, I have no right to ask you that."

"I resent losing Chillenden, but I try not to blame Papa. He did his best, which is all anyone can do. We all have our own burdens to bear."

A burden shared is a burden halved, he thought, but it was neither the time nor the place to speak out. He asked her about her father, trying to understand the man who was in part responsible for the existence of the woman he loved.

Love had crept up on him unawares. As he carried her, tired, trusting, back up the stairs later, he mused on the course of their acquaintance. It had all started with his gratitude for the help of a chance-met stranger in a country inn; now that stranger was in his arms, and he never wanted to let her go.

Reluctantly he left her in Miss Pinkerton's care and went downstairs. There was work to be done.

Mr. Deakins had left on his desk in the estate office the bills for the repairs to his tenants' farms. Harsh reality intruded on his dreams. His bank balance, having swelled remarkably as the proceeds of the harvest came in, had shrunk again after paying the servants' wages on Michaelmas quarter day. There were new saplings to be bought, men to be paid for felling and planting and pruning. A feeling of panic assailed him at the prospect of losing Millicent's twenty thousand pounds.

She had been assiduously attentive to Mr. Ruddle throughout their visit. Had she decided to take the bird in the hand? Had she guessed at his feelings for her cousin?

Chris cursed himself for a coward. He would manage without the dowry. He could never be satisfied with Millicent when he loved Rowena, even if he could not afford to ask her to be his wife. He settled down to serious calculations, covering sheet after sheet of paper with figures and lists in his neat handwriting.

Hours passed before he ruled two black lines at the bottom of the last page. He gathered up the sheaf of papers and went to see Lady Farleigh.

"Her ladyship is dressing for dinner, my lord. I was about to take the liberty of sending to remind your lordship of the time."

"Thank you, Diggory. I do vaguely remember someone coming in and lighting the lamps an hour or two since."

Chris went upstairs. He paused outside Rowena's door. He wanted desperately to see her, but she was probably alone, for she no longer needed a constant nurse, and Miss Pinkerton also must be dressing for dinner.

He knocked, anyway.

"Who is it?" She sounded drowsy.

"It's Chris."

"Come in."

She was reclining on the chaise longue by the fireplace, the flickering light of the flames drawing red-gold gleams from her tousled hair. She blinked up at him, a dreamy smile curving her lips.

"I did not mean to wake you. I just wanted to be sure that you have not suffered from going below stairs this morning." Torn between his desire to gather her into his arms and his knowledge that he should not be there, he was awkward.

"I was not really asleep."

"I meant to come and see you sooner, but I was working."

"I know. Mrs. Diggory came in to see if I needed anything, and she told me you'd been closeted in your office all afternoon."

"There is so much to do."

"Is there any way I can help?"

Once again it was the wrong moment to tell her he wanted her beside him to help him forever. He must not stay, and he had to talk to Lady Farleigh before he dared commit himself.

"Only by taking care of yourself and making a quick recovery. I must go." He could not resist raising her soft, warm, little hand to his lips and pressing a kiss in the palm.

She flushed fiery red, and as he left he thought he heard her murmur, "I must be dreaming still."

With a tender smile and a dream in his own grey eyes, he went at last to change for dinner.

Lady Farleigh adamantly refused to spend the evening talking business. "In the morning, dear boy," she said. "You may come to my sitting room at nine. And don't look so surprised, I may not appear below stairs until eleven but I assure you it is my habit to rise at a reasonable hour."

Chris laughed, thinking how lucky he was to have inherited her along with the Grange. He had no qualms about opening his budget to her tomorrow. Instead of the vapours, or sulks, or tantrum he might expect from a lesser woman, she would give him her honest opinion.

When he presented himself next morning, she was already busy writing letters. Her sitting room was no elegant, feminine boudoir but a comfortable, rather old-fashioned place, a strong contrast to the splendour of the rest of the house.

"I would not let Farleigh furnish this for me," she said, noting his surprise. "Sheraton and Hepplewhite have their place, but an old lady must have somewhere to relax. I look forward to removing to the Dower House. You have not seen it, I think. It is a charming Queen Anne house."

"I have ridden by it, ma'am. Is it in good condition?"

"Farleigh renovated it when I would not let him pull it down and rebuild from nothing. Miss Pinkerton and I shall be very comfortable there. I trust you mean to marry Miss Caxton soon?"

"How do you...? It seems everyone knows my mind before I know it myself! I have not asked her yet. I have so little to offer her, for we shall have to cut expenses to the bone to manage at all, if indeed it can be done. That is what I want to ask you about."

Lady Farleigh had all the household expenses at her fingertips. She knew which of the servants could easily find a new place and which had been with the family for years and must stay on, or go with her to the Dower House. She was full of suggestions as to which parts of the vast mansion might most easily be closed up, and which expensive pieces of furniture might be sold profitably and never missed. Chris scribbled notes and numbers and referred to yesterday's calculations, and at last he set down his pen with a sigh.

"It can be done. It is not what I should like to give her."

"Do you think Miss Caxton cares whether she lives in the style of a countess?"

"No, but I had hoped to offer her more."

"Silly boy, offer her your heart. That is all she wants."

Chris went away comforted and hopeful. He went straight to Rowena's door, where he was told firmly by Miss Pinkerton that he could not possibly enter for at least an hour. He sought out Bernard in the library.

The captain was seated at the vast mahogany desk, engaged in his own lists and calculations.

"We shall live with Cousin Martha for some time while I show her London," he announced as Chris entered. "Then we shall travel. I cannot wait to explore Paris and Rome and Vienna with her."

"You have come to an understanding, then?" Chris dropped into one of the large, leather-covered chairs and lounged back.

"With Anne, yes. She is the dearest girl! I have to ask Sir Henry's permission, and then I must post up to London to tell Cousin Martha. I think it best to deliver the news in person, do not you?"

"Certainly, if you mean to billet yourselves upon her."

"On the contrary, she would be shocked and horrified if I were to suggest taking a house elsewhere in town."

"And Anne has no objection?"

"She thinks it a delightful plan, especially as she need not trouble her head about housekeeping. We shall visit all the libraries and bookshops and museums and—"

"Enough! You are very sure of Sir Henry's consent."

Bernard shrugged. "I am no earl, to be sure, but my birth is as respectable as his and my means are adequate to support his daughter in comfort, if not in luxury. Martha's house will be mine eventually, you know. Anne may spend her couple of thousand on books with my good will. I expect Sir Henry's consent, but does he choose to withhold it, I shall run away with her."

"Bernard! I always thought you the most conventional of men."

"We love each other, and I shall not let anything stand in our way. Surely you can understand that?"

"Yes, I suppose so." Chris's voice was dubious. He adored Rowena, and he hoped that she was fond of him, but he had no assurance of mutual love to buoy him. His discovery of his feelings was too recent to have allowed time to delve into the implications, especially as purely practical considerations had come first. Would he risk the scandal that must attach to a runaway marriage? He was not sure, so it was fortunate that Rowena was her own mistress. On the other hand, he was once more overcome with doubts as to whether it was honourable to ask her to share what must amount, for some years at least, to hard work and straitened circumstances.

Bernard was talking. "She and Lady Grove are coming this morning to take Rowena home. The house is bound to be in something of an upset, so I shall ride over tomorrow to speak to her father."

"This morning? I promised to send her home in my carriage, filled with pillows, and I have done nothing about it. Potter shall go with them." To escort her himself on such a short drive would look excessively particular. He jumped up and strode to the door, then turned and said thoughtfully, "I'll ride with you tomorrow."

It was too late to speak to Rowena this morning, and this afternoon she would be tired from the journey.

Tomorrow, in her aunt's house, he would lay before her all the disadvantages of becoming his wife, and he would find out whether the offer of his heart was compensation enough.

CHAPTER SEVENTEEN

"I WISH YOU HAD let me get up earlier, Pinkie!" wailed Rowena. "Now he will think I don't want to see him." She was sitting in a copper hip bath before the fire, carefully shielded from draughts by a pair of Chinese screens, with her hair full of soapsuds and her eyes screwed shut.

"Nonsense, child, he is not such a slowtop as to suppose it must always be convenient for a lady to receive him in her chamber."

"He is not a slowtop at all, but I am going back to my aunt's today."

"And that is precisely why I did not let you rise early. A fine thing it would be if you were worn out before your aunt comes to fetch you. Now bend your head while I rinse your hair or you will have soap in your eyes."

Rowena leaned forward obediently. It hardly hurt to move any more, and it felt wonderful to be clean all over. All the same, once she had stepped out of the bath to be enveloped in a huge, well-warmed towel, she was ready to lie quietly by the fire while her hair dried.

Miss Pinkerton bustled about the room, humming as she packed the few clothes that had been brought down from Grove Park.

"I wish you were coming, too," said Rowena suddenly.

"Lady Farleigh says I may borrow a carriage whenever I wish to visit you, my love. And besides, I daresay it will not be long before you return."

"Do you really think so? I wish I could be certain. He needs money so badly, Pinkie, and I have nothing to give him. If he does...does want to marry me, perhaps I ought to refuse so that he can have Millie."

"Fustian, my girl, would you condemn him to a fate worse than death?"

This drew a reluctant chuckle from Rowena, but she quickly sobered. "I love him too much to say no if he asks me, even though we both may regret it later. I wish I had a huge dowry to give him."

"Be glad you don't, Rowena. At least you will know, if he offers for you, that it is you he loves and not your money."

"Like Millicent and Mr. Ruddle."

"Precisely. The girl is a fool if she does not take him."

Rowena thought of Pinkie's words when Chris came to carry her down to the carriage. When he lifted her in his arms, she felt his tension, and the look he gave her was searching, troubled. She clasped her hands behind his neck and pressed herself against him in an effort to reassure him. If his worry had nothing to do with her, if she had misinterpreted the message in his eyes yesterday, he would think her shockingly forward. She was willing to risk it.

Though his arms tightened about her, he seemed to relax a little.

"The carriage is so full of cushions, I am not sure there is room left for you," he said teasingly, "especially as your cousin thinks you will prefer company instead of riding in solitary state."

"And is my aunt to squeeze in, too?"

"I understand she was delayed by unexpected visitors. Anne was too impatient to wait, and she is at this moment receiving a scold from Bernard for riding down with only a groom to escort her. She sent the groom home with a message to Lady Grove that she need not come. I ought to have informed everyone yesterday that you had accepted the offer of my carriage, but I had other matters on my mind."

Rowena longed to ask for an explanation of those other matters, but they had reached the bottom of the stair. Lady Farleigh was waiting there, with Miss Pinkerton, Bernard, and Anne, who looked less than cowed by her scolding. Chris set Rowena lightly on her feet, and she performed a somewhat wobbly curtsy, glad of his strong arm to grasp as she rose.

"My lady, I cannot thank you sufficiently for your hospitality."

"It was nothing, Miss Caxton." Lady Farleigh waved dismissal, then added severely, "However, I trust you will honour me with a visit when you have recovered your strength, without waiting for your aunt to bring you."

"Of course, ma'am, I shall be happy to." Rowena smiled at the dowager, aware by now that her sharp manner hid a warm heart.

Pinkie hugged her and kissed her cheek and promised to call at Grove Park tomorrow. The captain wished her a short convalescence, and it was time to go. Rowena was suddenly struck with embarrassment at the thought of everyone watching as Chris picked her up and carried her out.

"I shall walk," she told him with dignity, "if you will lend me your support?"

"Now what would you do if I said no?" he asked wickedly, but he offered his arm, and when she laid her hand on it, he covered it with his own.

Her progress was halting, and by the time they reached the bottom of the front steps she was leaning on him heavily, but she managed.

The effort was amply repaid when he said softly, "You are indomitable, Rowena. May I call tomorrow?"

"Oh, yes, please do. I...I shall be happy to see you."

Without waiting for permission he swung her off her feet and deposited her on a mound of cushions in the carriage. There were velvet cushions and brocade, cushions trimmed with lace, embroidered, tapestry-covered, plain satin and striped, in every colour of the rainbow. Anne hopped in, blowing a kiss to Bernard without the least regard for propriety, and settled on the opposite seat. The carriage rumbled into motion.

Rowena burst into tears.

Anne looked at her in astonished horror. She dropped to her knees on the joggling floor of the coach and put her arms round her cousin.

"Darling Rowena, whatever is the matter?"

"It's just that he—that everyone is so kind," she sobbed.

"You must be tired. That's nothing to cry about."

"I know, I can't help it, and I can't find my handkerchief."

"Here's mine." Anne returned to her seat. "I'm glad you're not crying because you are miserable, for I am positively bursting to tell someone. Bernard is coming tomorrow to ask Papa for my hand!"

"Oh, Anne, I am so glad. I know I need not wish you happy." Rowena dried her eyes and did her best to enter into her cousin's elation. She was truly delighted, but she could not help wishing that she dared reciprocate with the news that Chris was on the point of offering for her. Though her heart told her it was true, her head kept reminding her that Millicent was beautiful and rich, and she was neither.

They had turned in at the gates of Grove Park before Anne's euphoria abated enough for her to recall a matter of minor interest.

"A letter came for you this morning. It looked to me like your lawyer's hand. Do you suppose he has found another hundred pounds for you? What will you spend it on?"

"I'll cross that bridge when I come to it, instead of counting my chickens before they hatch. I hope it is not a request to send back the hundred pounds to pay a newly discovered debt."

"How fortunate that you have already spent half of it."

"Goosecap, it is probably just another paper to be signed, like most of his communications."

"I suppose so. Don't tell Mama and Millie that Bernard is coming tomorrow, will you? I must tell Papa, of course, so that he will be there, but I want a *fait accompli* before Millie finds out."

Rowena reassured her, as the carriage drew up before the front door. Potter appeared from nowhere to let down the step. He helped Anne down and turned to Rowena.

"The major's orders was to carry you in, miss, but I seen you walk out o' there like a Trojan, so if you'd rather take me arm, like?"

"You are willing to disobey the major for me, corporal?"

He grinned at her. "You won't never give me away, miss."

"To be sure I shall not. Yes, I prefer to walk, thank you. Pray tell his lordship that I have never had so restful a journey in my life."

Even after walking in, Rowena felt well enough to sit for a while in the parlour instead of retiring at once to bed. She was ensconced in a comfortable chair by the fire, and Anne brought a footstool while Aunt Hermione rang for tea to restore her. With the tea tray, the butler brought her the letter.

"Go ahead and read it, child," said Lady Grove. "No need to stand upon ceremony when there are none but family here, though I expect Mr. Ruddle will bring Millicent back presently."

The direction was in Mr. Harwin's hand, and the paper was sealed with the usual mass of wax. Fortunately the butler had provided a paper knife. Rowena slit the seal, unfolded two sheets and began to read. It seemed only polite to inform her companions of the contents as she went along.

"I explained, did I not, Aunt, about the confusion Papa's papers were in? It seems Mr. Harwin's clerk has at last finished going through them. Most are unimportant, receipts and such. He lists them but I will not bore you with such stuff. 'There is one, however...'" She turned to the next page. "'...which proves beyond a doubt that a large portion of the mortgage on Chillenden Manor was paid long since. I have taken the liberty of resolving the matter with the lender before informing you of the result. I beg to inform you, my dear Miss Caxton, that I am holding for you from the proceeds of the sale of Chillenden the sum of ten thousand, two hundred..." The words swam before Rowena's eyes.

"Mama, she is fainting! Where are your smelling salts? Pray ring for some brandy. Rowena! Oh, you are horridly pale. Rowena, it is *good* news. Listen, I will read it to you." With the hand that was not waving the vinaigrette, Anne snatched up the letter. "Here's the place. 'My dear Miss Caxton, I am holding for you' et-cetera 'the sum of ten thousand, two hundred and forty four pounds, six shillings and sixpence.' Rowena, that is a fortune!"

"Ten thousand pounds!" Millicent had entered the room unnoticed, followed by Mr. Ruddle. "Rowena cannot possibly have so much. Her papa died a pauper."

"Well, she does," crowed Anne, triumphing over her sister for once. "Here is her lawyer's letter. It is down in black and white." She hesitated a moment, but the opportunity was too splendid to miss. "And not only is Rowena rich, but I am going to be betrothed to Captain Cartwright!"

"Betrothed!" Millicent's voice rose to a shriek. "Mama, I will not have it. The disgrace of my younger sister engaged before me! It is out of the question. Papa must refuse him."

"Really, Millicent, do not be shatterbrained! There can be no question of refusing the match, if your papa is satisfied with the captain's ability to support dear Anne."

Millicent gaped at her mother in shock, then burst into tears.

Rowena let the storm rage over her head. With trembling fingers she retrieved the letter from the floor where Anne had let it fall, smoothed it and reread the staggering news. Though she had recovered from her momentary dizziness, it still left her breathless. If Chris indeed loved and wanted her, she need have no qualms about accepting. With ten thousand pounds, Farleigh Grange could be set to rights and turned into the productive estate it ought to be.

Her attention was drawn back to the combatants by a portentous clearing of the throat. Mr. Ruddle, hitherto a distressed spectator, had decided to take a hand.

"My dear Miss Grove," he began, a solemn look on his round, pink face, "do not be discomposed, I beg you. Miss Grove—Millicent, if I may be so bold—allow me to offer—not for the first time!—my hand and heart. It is my dearest wish—and has been these two years and more—to make you my wife and the mistress of Ruddle Towers. If you will only say yes, I shall seek out Sir Henry this instant and we may be formally betrothed before dinner. I have the ring here, next to my heart as always, waiting for you to relent." He delved into a waistcoat pocket and produced a diamond the size of a gooseberry.

"Pray do, Millicent!" begged her mother, herself near tears.

"Heavens!" gasped Anne, her gaze on the gem. "I thought only the Crown Jewels had diamonds so enormous. I've never seen anything like it."

"It is superb, is it not?" said her sister graciously. "I fear you cannot expect anything of the sort from a half-pay officer. Dear Mr. Ruddle, I feel it is time I rewarded your constancy. Papa is probably in his study at this hour."

"I shall go at once." The dandy kissed his beloved's hand reverently, delighted at this sudden turn. "You have made me the happiest man in the world."

"I expect he may be," Anne murmured to Rowena, "for he will never even notice her megrims. Every time she throws a tantrum he will give her another diamond."

Mr. Ruddle left and Millicent turned to Rowena. "So you have inherited ten thousand?" she enquired. "I am happy for you."

Anne and Rowena exchanged startled glances.

"Is it not delightful?" Lady Grove beamed. "Rowena must have a Season. With such a marriage portion she may look for a husband as high as you please. And both my daughters betrothed! I believe I shall call on Lady Amelia. Anne, ring the bell, pray, and order the carriage."

Her ladyship went off to spread the good news about the neighbourhood. Rowena, exhausted, stumbled upstairs on the footman's arm and sank into her bed. A Season in London! She had not even considered the possibility. But what was the point of a Season when she had already found the only husband she would ever want.

CHAPTER EIGHTEEN

CHRIS AND BERNARD were ushered into the front hall at Grove Park as the clock struck eleven. Anne rushed out of the morning parlour, her face alight with joyous anticipation.

"Papa is in his study. Come quick."

"I daresay he will not mind waiting while I take off my coat." Despite his prosaic words, Bernard's tone was warm, his expression near as eager as hers, as he handed his hat and gloves to the butler.

Belatedly recalling her manners, Anne turned to Chris, already divested of his topcoat by a footman. She curtsied. "Good morning, my lord. Mama and Millie are in the parlour, and I believe Rowena will be down directly."

"And you can escort Chris, sweet ... Miss Anne, for I must speak alone with Sir Henry," said the captain firmly.

Irrepressible, she stood on tiptoe and planted a kiss on his cheek. "He promised to be nice to you. He has to be, for Mama already told Lady Amelia, so half the county knows by now."

Shaking his head with a grin, Bernard went off. Chris offered his arm to Anne and she laid her fingertips on it, suddenly the regal lady. They moved towards the parlour.

"How is Rowena?" he asked. "I trust the journey did not prove too tiring?"

"No, not with your mountains of cushions to rest on. It was the excitement afterwards that exhausted her, but she is quite well and I know she means to come down."

"Excitement?"

"Such news! And then Millie... But she will want to tell you herself. Mama, here is Lord Farleigh."

"My lady, Miss Grove." Chris bowed, hoping his apprehension at Anne's hints was not obvious. "I hope I see you well, ma'am."

"Oh, yes, my lord, prodigious well. I vow I do not know when I have been better. Only think, all my girls, and all on the same day... I do not know whether I am on my head or my heels, I do declare."

"You refer to Miss Anne's betrothal, I collect? My friend is speaking to Sir Henry on that account at this moment."

"To be sure. I cannot claim to know Captain Cartwright well, but an admirable gentleman, without a doubt, and a friend of yours, of course, my lord. And then Millicent! You must know that she has at last accepted dear Mr. Ruddle, who has been a faithful beau ever since her come-out."

Chris turned to Millicent, half relieved to know that her fortune was now beyond his reach though he had decided he could manage without it. "I must wish you happy, Miss Grove, and I hope soon to have the opportunity of congratulating the lucky man."

"Thank you, my lord. We expect Mr. Ruddle at any moment."

Millicent waved her fan languidly in such a way as to ensure his noticing the huge diamond on her ring finger. Chris was left with the impression that if he chose to throw his handkerchief, preferably embellished with jewels, in her direction, he need not despair despite her betrothal. He hoped he did not do her justice. The thought of Rowena was like a draught of clear, cool water after a sticky-sweet sherbet.

Then, with a shock of dismay, he recalled Lady Grove's words.

"You said, all your girls, did not you? What of Miss Caxton, ma'am?" Surely she was not betrothed, too!

"Now that is of all things the most surprising and the most delightful! Dearest Rowena turns out to be quite an heiress after all, a most respectable portion. With Anne off my hands, I shall take her up to town in the spring, for she may expect now to make a most eligible connexion. Indeed, I venture to say she may look for a splendid match."

The arrival of Mr. Ruddle, Mrs. Berry-Browning and her son saved Chris from the necessity of responding. He managed to utter polite greetings, but his mind was in a whirl.

His immediate reaction to the news was joy. Though Rowena's aunt, with unusual reticence, had not mentioned a figure, a respectable fortune could only ease their life together. He would not have to ask her to do without the elegancies he longed to provide.

Second thoughts came all too soon. The world would think that having lost Millicent's dowry, he had seized the chance of securing Rowena's before anyone else learned of it. They would whisper pityingly that he had only married her for her money. The very day he heard the news, they would say, he offered for her, and never a hint before that he had eyes for any but Millicent Grove and her twenty thousand.

The worst of it was that Rowena might believe it. The more he tried to convince her of his love, the more she must doubt his sincerity. How could he face the questions in her green eyes?

He cursed himself for not begging her to marry him before she left the Grange.

Yet if he had, and if she had accepted, the only honourable course of action now would be to free her from her promise. Lady Grove was talking of a London Season, the height of every young lady's ambition, and of a splendid match. All Chris had to offer was a run-down estate and a great deal of hard work.

The unpleasant reality was impossible to ignore: he could not ask Rowena to be his wife.

Several more visitors arrived to discover for themselves the details of Lady Grove's triumph, which had quickly spread about the neighbourhood. Bernard appeared with Sir Henry, both beaming. Anne and her captain were surrounded immediately by well-wishers. Then Rowena came in.

She paused in the doorway, glancing about the room. In the moment before she caught sight of him, Chris saw that she looked well, with a becoming colour in her cheeks. Not daring to meet her eyes, he looked hastily away from her face. Her slight figure, clad in a gown of her favourite green, seemed vulnerable, defenseless. He ached to hold her, to protect her.

He turned away to answer Miss Desborough. When he looked back, Rowena was the centre of a congratulatory group.

With a rush of jealous fury he noted that Mr. Desborough and Mr. Berry-Browning were both hovering about her with a hopeful air. He must leave before he did something he would regret. Bidding his hostess farewell, he told Bernard he would see him later and made his way to Rowena.

The glow in her green eyes when she looked up at him almost made him forget his resolution. It was only pleasure at the unusual attention she was receiving, he told himself. He bowed over the hand she held out to him, not touching it.

"My felicitations, Miss Caxton." His voice sounded strange to his own ears.

Her smile faded. "Thank you, my lord."

"You must excuse me, I have business to attend to." With a nod to the other members of her circle, he departed.

He rode long and hard over the hills in a vain attempt to drive her image from his mind. Everything reminded him of her.

It was sunny, though the October breeze had a nip to it—a perfect day for a gallop, and Rowena loved a good gallop. How alarmed he had been when he had found her weeping over her mare—had he loved her even then, unknowingly? Would she go back now to Geoffrey Farnhouse, who was fond enough of her to buy her horse and send it to her? Her denial of interest in him as anything more than a friend had seemed convincing, but perhaps it was wishful thinking on his part.

He swung over the crest of a hill, scattering a flock of sheep. They turned to look at him with reproachful eyes. *I did it for the best,* he wanted to shout at them; *it would be dishonourable to ask her to marry me.*

The shepherd's tuneless whistle brought memories of joking about their mutual lack of musical appreciation.

Even the innocent grass was green, her favourite colour.

By the time he reached the Grange stables, El Cid was near exhaustion, and the return through the orchards had set the seal on Chris's misery. Those had been his happiest times with Rowena, riding among the trees discussing his improvements. Was he to lose even the benefit of her advice?

He strode into the house, scowling. The dome over the magnificent vestibule was just another reminder that bricks and mortar had stolen his inheritance and his beloved from him.

"Her ladyship desires a word with your lordship," announced Diggory.

"Later," said the earl curtly.

He managed to avoid Lady Farleigh and Miss Pinkerton until dinnertime. Bernard had still not returned from Grove Park. However, a number of callers had dropped in at the Grange, bringing with them the news of Lady Grove's triple triumph. Chris spun out his description of the captain's successful wooing, and to his relief the ladies refrained from interrogating him further, though he knew they were agog to hear about Rowena. The dowager had made it plain enough that she would welcome Miss Caxton as a surrogate daughter-in-law.

Chris sat long at the table after the ladies had withdrawn. He had never appreciated the rich sweetness of port but the level in the brandy decanter sank considerably before Bernard joined him.

Though it was hard to focus, he noted with annoyance the spring in his friend's step, negating his limp.

"Take a spot?" he mumbled as Diggory materialized with another glass.

"Just a drop of the port." Bernard studied Chris's face and wisely forbore from comment. "Thank you. I leave for London first thing tomorrow."

"Want to bring Cousin Martha back...meet your betrothed?"

"May I? That would be ideal, for Lady Grove cannot be spared to accompany Anne to town."

"Welcome. What time we leaving?"

"I hope to be off by half past seven. With luck I'll make it in a day. There's no need for you to come with me, Chris. I am perfectly well, never felt better in fact. I shall hire a post chaise in Broadway."

"I'm going, too," said Chris flatly.

The gentlemen were long gone when Miss Pinkerton set off next morning for Grove Park. It was a little after ten when she was ushered up to Rowena's chamber.

Rowena was sitting at a small table, writing. With unshaken composure she set aside her pen, but when she embraced Pinkie her hug was convulsive. "You are quite chilled! Sit down here by the fire and let me help you take off your bonnet. There, that's better, but your cap is awry, and I never thought to see you tousled."

"One of the grooms was kind enough to bring me in the gig. Lady Farleigh does not keep another carriage and I could not like to borrow his lordship's curricle. Such a sporting vehicle! The travelling carriage was gone, you see. His lordship and the captain left for London at dawn."

Rowena nodded sadly. "I thought he would go with Bernard."

"What happened, my love?"

"I don't know." She stood up again and restlessly paced the room. "There were a number of people there when I went down. He was on the other side of the room. I knew something was wrong as soon as I saw his face. So stern and unhappy! He spoke scarce two words to me before he left. I hoped he might come back when there were no visitors, but when he did not, I knew he would go to London. I can only suppose that he really does love Millicent, that her betrothal was the cause of his distress." Rowena sank to her knees and buried her face in Miss Pinkerton's skirts, though no tears came. "Oh, Pinkie, I did think he was beginning to care for me!"

"So did I, my dear." Pinkie gently stroked her hair. "I trust that nothing I said raised your hopes above what was warranted. Lady Farleigh, too, fears that she may have encouraged you beyond reason."

"It was he, his actions, his looks, that gave me encouragement. How could I have mistaken him so? And yet I cannot think him dishonourable. I saw what I wanted to see, I daresay. What a fool I have been!"

"He is the greater fool!" said Miss Pinkerton in indignation. "He'll not find himself a better wife if he looks for a thousand years."

Rowena stood up, went over to the table, and began to mend her pen. "I wish I could be gone before he returns. I cannot go on living so close. I expect my aunt and Sir Henry will not approve, but I have written to Mr. Harwin to ask him how to go about buying or renting a little farm. Will you come to live with me?"

"I should be grossly offended if I thought for a minute you doubted it, Rowena. A neat, small farm will be the very thing to occupy your mind. What a delightful notion!"

"You are not promised to Lady Farleigh?"

"No, no, our plans were all contingent upon . . . that is, I daresay she will continue at the Grange for the foreseeable future."

"Then I shall send this letter today." She folded the sheet, directed and sealed it. "It may take some little time for Mr. Harwin to reply."

For the next few days, while awaiting the lawyer's response, Rowena did her best to appear cheerful. She supported Anne's spirits during Bernard's absence; she listened to Millicent's descriptions of the luxurious life she would lead as "dear Adolphus'" wife; she tactfully discouraged Aunt Hermione's preparations for a London Season without revealing her own plans.

Sure that Lord Farleigh must have guessed her feelings, she dreaded his reappearance. She recalled with shame how she had hung on his neck and pressed against him when he carried her. He had been kind enough not to show his disgust at her want of conduct—or had he been amused? That would almost be worse.

She never wanted to see him again.

CHAPTER NINETEEN

"ROWENA, *pray* come to the Grange with me. How can I possibly meet Miss Cartwright without your support? She is Bernard's only living relative and he is excessively fond of her. I am so dreadfully afraid she will not like me."

Curled up at the foot of Rowena's bed, Anne let slip the eiderdown wrapped about her thin shoulders as she waved the brief note from her beloved to emphasize her plea.

"I did not know he meant to bring her back with him." Rowena tried to postpone the moment of decision.

"Nor did he, before he left. He says Chris suggested it. Was it not kind of him?"

She ignored the question. "Could you not invite Miss Cartwright to come up here?"

"I think it would be more proper for me to go to her." Anne looked dubious. "Bernard does ask me to go."

"Yes, of course, you are right, but surely Aunt Hermione ought to go with you."

"I daresay, but you know very well Millie has talked her into going to Cheltenham tomorrow to order brideclothes. I know you are not quite recovered, but if I send word to Bernard first thing tomorrow that we shall not have the carriage, I'm sure Chris will send his for us. Perhaps he will fill it with cushions again."

She giggled. Rowena winced. Unable to explain how unlikely that was, she capitulated.

"I'll go with you."

"Good. Let's not tell Millie they are back or she will want to come, too. Though I must say she seems quite happy to be engaged to dear Adolphus. I wish she had taken the plunge sooner, for her disposition is much improved, is it not? All the same, we shall say we are going to see your Pinkie."

Rowena scarcely slept that night for planning what she would say to Lord Farleigh if she were forced to speak to him. Nor could she decide what to wear. In one of her pretty new dresses she might give the impression that she was trying to attract him, yet she could not bear to go back to her old, shabby half-mourning. Besides, it would look excessively odd and provoke no end of comment.

When morning came and she had to make up her mind, she settled after all on the moss-green Circassian cloth trimmed with peach. It hung loose on her, for she had lost weight since her accident, and it made her pale face look still paler. She stared crossly at her image in the mirror, then shrugged.

Bernard came in the Farleigh carriage to fetch the girls. He and Anne were too preoccupied with each other to note Rowena's apprehensive silence.

Lady Farleigh and Pinkie awaited them in the green-and-gold drawing room. With them was a motherly, cheerful woman whom Bernard introduced as his cousin Martha Cartwright. Rowena murmured greetings and curtsied, trying not to let her gaze wander about the room in search of his lordship.

Her efforts were unnecessary. He was not there. He must have gone riding to avoid her.

She sought refuge beside Pinkie, and did her best to take an interest in the conversation. Bernard was looking wary. Anne's intellectual pursuits and sometimes sharp tongue accorded ill with Miss Cartwright's comfortable common sense, and for a time a clash seemed inevitable. However, with a little nudging from Pinkie and Lady Farleigh they quickly found a mutual interest in their adoration of the captain, to that gentleman's patent embarrassment.

The girls were invited to stay for luncheon. Lord Farleigh had still not put in an appearance.

"Now, how am I to escort five ladies into the dining room?" said Bernard, laughing. "I ought to have insisted that Chris return with me to perform his duties as host."

"Is he still in London?" Anne asked the question that hovered on Rowena's tongue.

"He went down to Dorset, to see his sister." He offered his arm to Lady Farleigh, as the first in precedence and most in need. "He is very fond of her, and of all his nephews and nieces, too, and he has seen little of them since we returned to England."

Rowena trailed after the others into the dining room. She was not hungry. Bernard might explain Chris's absence by his affection for his sister, but she was afraid it was her presence nearby that had driven him from his home.

Miss Cartwright stayed for a week. The day after Bernard accompanied her back to town, Rowena received from an agent in Evesham a list of four local properties he thought suitable for her purposes. She disclosed her plans to the Groves. Their reactions were exactly what she might have expected.

Millicent was utterly incredulous at the very notion of choosing to become a farmer instead of a debutante. Aunt Hermione wailed about the impropriety of a young lady leaving her family to live alone. Sir Henry told her she must do as she saw fit. Anne was both encouraging and practical.

"You will have to inspect all the farms to see which you like best," she pointed out. "I shall go with you, since Bernard is away. Papa, may we have the carriage tomorrow?"

So, early the next morning the two young ladies set out on a tour of inspection, dressed in sensible warm clothes and boots suitable for walking about a farmyard. It was a perfect October day, still and sunny with a hint of frost in the air. Woods and orchards were dressed in autumn russet and gold; in the hedgerows flocks of chaffinches squabbled over the crimson haws.

Neither her cheerful companion nor the prospect of once again running her own farm could rouse Rowena to enthusiasm.

The first place, somewhere north of Evesham between Salford Priors and Abbot's Salford, was in excellent heart, but given over to sheep and cattle and grain. The second was planted to fruit trees, only they were in even worse condition than those at Farleigh Grange, and the house was a dilapidated shack. By the time they turned south, Rowena's dream of independence and a quiet, useful life was fading as the dream of winning Chris's love had faded.

"The next is bound to be better," Anne encouraged her. "Besides, you would not want to live in a village called Wyre Piddle."

Rowena summoned up a smile. "Hinton on the Green has a solid, respectable sound," she agreed, "and there has been nothing but orchards for some way. Are you sure your papa's coachman understood the directions to the farm? We seem to have been driving for... Oh, what is that?"

A shout was followed by a confused sound of cursing as the coach came to a sudden halt.

"Highwaymen!" Anne's eyes sparkled with excitement.

Rowena let down the window and looked out. "I'm sorry to disappoint you, but it seems to be Bernard. Oh, and Lord Farleigh!" She ducked back into the carriage as Anne flung open the door and jumped out.

What was Chris doing here? A moment's reflection told her that he had simply accompanied Bernard, who must have been impatient to see his betrothed.

She heard him now, talking to the coachman, at first apologetic then in a no-nonsense tone of command, his "major" voice. She could not make out his words. A moment later he led El Cid and Sluggard past the window towards the back of the carriage, presumably to tie them on behind, for he next appeared without them at the open door.

Of all the high-handed, arrogant wretches, to assume that she would want to ride with him!

"Good day, Miss Caxton." He doffed his hat and bowed, his dark hair ruffled by the breeze.

She saw uncertainty in his grey eyes, and her resentment melted. After all it was Anne's carriage. As Bernard's friend, Chris could hardly be refused a place in it.

"Good day, my lord."

"I beg your pardon if we caused you any alarm. I had not thought that your coachman might take us for highwaymen."

"I did not for a moment credit it. However, I trust we shall not be much longer delayed for I have two more farms to look at this afternoon."

"Ah, yes. As it happens, Bernard and I have already done some inspecting and have decided that the next is not at all what you will like. I know of the ideal place for you. In fact, I have taken the liberty of directing your coachman, in the hope that you will be so kind as to take me up so that I may show it to you."

His look was so appealing that she could not resist. Besides, her curiosity as to what he considered suitable was almost as great as her chagrin that he should fall in so readily with her plans for the future.

"Very well," she said gruffly.

He called to Anne and Bernard, who took their places close together on the facing seat. Rowena saw that they were holding hands. She blushed and pressed herself farther into the corner as Lord Farleigh sat down beside her. Suddenly he seemed very large. The carriage moved on.

"How did you know where we were?" Anne asked.

"Chris tracked you down," Bernard told her, "and not without considerable hazard. I regret to tell you, sweetheart, that when we went to enquire after you, your sister flung herself into Chris's arms and offered to send Mr. Ruddle to the rightabout, though I must admit it was in a half-hearted way."

"What a peagoose she is! She is perfectly happy with dear Adolphus, but I suppose the prospect of losing the title forever overcame her. Millie is a constant source of mortification to me. Whatever did Lord Farleigh do?"

"Why, to tell the truth I believe he scarcely noticed, eager as he was to find out which direction you had taken. I'd have been perfectly content to await your return at home."

"You should not have ridden so far! You must take better care of yourself," cried Anne.

Rowena had lost interest in their exchange. She stole a peek at Chris.

He was looking at her seriously. "Miss Pinkerton told me you had chosen not to go to London in the spring. That is, she told me you were seeking a farm to live on."

As an explanation it left a lot to be desired. Rowena could not think of any answer but a weak "Oh."

The engaged couple had a great deal to say to each other, but between Chris and Rowena conversation languished. She gazed out of the window as if fascinated by the passing scene, though she could not have said whether the hedges were hawthorn or hazel, whether the cottages of Hinton on the Green were built of stone or brick.

He had rejected her cousin. Of course that was the only gentlemanly thing to do, whatever Millicent's feelings, since she was betrothed to another.

Why had he come to meet her? Why was he determined that she should see the farm he chose rather than those she had set out to see? Why was he sitting there in silence looking, as another stolen glance showed her, both discouraged and anxious?

The carriage turned right and Rowena recognized the road to Down Stanton. A horrid suspicion seized her. One of his tenants must have given notice and he wanted her to take over the farm. Though he did not care to marry her he needed the benefit of her advice and expertise. In a way it was flattering, but it did not tempt her in the least. In fact, it would be unbearable.

"We are going towards Farleigh Grange," she cried, turning to him. "I won't go any farther." She let down the window and called to the coachman to stop. There were tears in her eyes; she furiously blinked them away.

"Why not?" Chris sounded alarmed. "What's wrong?"

"I do not want to be your tenant."

Smiling wryly, he captured her agitated hands. "It is true I am not the best of landlords. However, that is precisely the opposite of what I hoped for. Rowena, I want to be *your* tenant—for life."

She looked at him in confusion.

Bernard exchanged a glance with Anne. "I think this is where we go for a stroll," he suggested, and helped her down into the lane.

"Rowena, what is wrong?" Chris demanded urgently.

"What does that mean, that you want to be my...tenant for life?"

"A reprehensible phrase signifying a husband. I want to be yours."

"Then why did you go away, stay away so long?"

"Because of your inheritance, and Millicent's betrothal. I knew what people would say, and I was afraid you would believe it. Besides, I thought you wanted to have your Season and make a splendid match."

"What people would say? Oh, I see!" It had not crossed her mind before, when she was so delighted to have the money to smooth his path, but people would talk. Millicent, for one, would be certain that Chris's offer was prompted by Rowena's unexpected inheritance. All her loving trust was in her eyes as she assured him, "But I do not care what people say."

"I decided I don't, either. I want you too much to give you up for such a silly reason. And you do not want a splendid match?"

"Oh, yes, I want to be a countess."

Chris tightened his grip on her hands and she moved a little closer, but still he held her away from him. "Rowena, I love you and I want more than anything in the world to marry you, but you know I cannot offer a life of luxury. Your money must be put in a trust fund for our children, so we shall have to scrape by as best we can."

His children! Rowena felt the colour rise in her cheeks. But what nonsense the dear man was talking.

"I mean to invest my fortune," she said with determination.

"Of course you shall choose how it shall be disposed." He looked disconcerted.

"The only investment with which I am conversant is agriculture," she continued demurely, hiding a smile. "I believe the best use that can be made of it is to improve a faltering estate so that in due course it will yield proper returns."

"Shall I never learn when you are roasting me? Come here."

"Yes, Major." She obeyed.

He swept her into his arms and stopped her mouth with his. The warm firmness of his lips, the pressure of his hands on her back, convinced her of his love.

Dizzy with happiness, clinging to him, she vaguely heard the sound of applause. Anne's and Bernard's faces appeared at the window.

"It looks as if she has accepted him," said Bernard.

"And about time too!" said Anne.

HARLEQUIN
American Romance®

RELIVE THE MEMORIES....

From New York's immigrant experience to San Francisco's Great Quake of '06. From the western front of World War I to the Roaring Twenties. From the indomitable spirit of the thirties to the home front of the Fabulous Forties to the baby-boom fifties...A CENTURY OF AMERICAN ROMANCE takes you on a nostalgic journey.

From the turn of the century to the dawn of the year 2000, you'll revel in the romance of a time gone by and sneak a peek at romance in an exciting future.

Watch for all the CENTURY OF AMERICAN ROMANCE titles coming to you one per month over the next four months in Harlequin American Romance.

Don't miss a day of A CENTURY OF AMERICAN ROMANCE.

A CENTURY OF
AMERICAN ROMANCE
1960s

The women...the men...the passions...the memories...

If you missed #345 AMERICAN PIE, #349 SATURDAY'S CHILD, #353 THE GOLDEN RAINTREE, #357 THE SENSATION, #361 ANGELS WINGS, #365 SENTIMENTAL JOURNEY or #369 STRANGER IN PARADISE and would like to order them, send your name, address, and zip or postal code along with a check or money order for $2.95 plus 75¢ for postage and handling ($1.00 in Canada) *for each book ordered*, Canadian residents add applicable federal and provincial taxes, payable to Harlequin Reader Service, to:

In the U.S.
3010 Walden Ave.
P.O. Box 1325
Buffalo, NY 14269-1325

In Canada
P.O. Box 609
Fort Erie, Ontario
L2A 5X3

Please specify book title with your order.

CA-60-R

You'll flip . . . your pages won't!
Read paperbacks *hands-free* with

Book Mate • I

The perfect "mate" for all your romance paperbacks

Traveling • Vacationing • At Work • In Bed • Studying • Cooking • Eating

Perfect size for all standard paperbacks, this wonderful invention makes reading a pure pleasure! Ingenious design holds paperback books OPEN and FLAT so even wind can't ruffle pages— leaves your hands free to do other things. Reinforced, wipe-clean vinyl-covered holder flexes to let you turn pages without undoing the strap . . . supports paperbacks so well, they have the strength of hardcovers!

Pages turn WITHOUT opening the strap

SEE-THROUGH STRAP

Reinforced back stays flat

Built in bookmark

BOOK MARK

BACK COVER HOLDING STRIP

10 x 7¼ opened
Snaps closed for easy carrying, too

Available now. Send your name, address, and zip code, along with a check or money order for just $5.95 + .75¢ for delivery (for a total of $6.70) payable to Reader Service to:

Reader Service
Bookmate Offer
3010 Walden Avenue
P.O. Box 1396
Buffalo, N.Y. 14269-1396

Offer not available in Canada
*New York residents add appropriate sales tax.

BM-GR

 *Harlequin Intrigue*®

REBECCA YORK

Labeled a "true master of intrigue" by *Rave Reviews*, best-selling author Rebecca York makes her Harlequin Intrigue debut with an exciting suspenseful new series.

43
Light St.

It looks like a charming old building near the renovated Baltimore waterfront, but inside 43 Light Street lurks danger . . . and romance.

Let Rebecca York introduce you to:

> *Abby Franklin*—a psychologist who risks everything to save a tough adventurer determined to find the truth about his sister's death. . . .
>
> *Jo O'Malley*—a private detective who finds herself matching wits with a serial killer who makes her his next target. . . .
>
> *Laura Roswell*—a lawyer whose inherited share in a development deal lands her in the middle of a murder. And she's the chief suspect. . . .

These are just a few of the occupants of 43 Light Street you'll meet in Harlequin Intrigue's new ongoing series. Don't miss any of the 43 LIGHT STREET books, beginning with #143 LIFE LINE.

And watch for future LIGHT STREET titles, including #155 SHATTERED VOWS (February 1991) and #167 WHISPERS IN THE NIGHT (August 1991).

From the author of
DADDY, DARLING

DOCTOR, DARLING
by
Glenda Sanders

The eagerly awaited sequel to DADDY,
DARLING is here! In DOCTOR, DARLING,
the imposing Dr. Sergei Karol meets his match.
He's head over heels in love with Polly
Mechler, the adorable TV celebrity whose
plumbing-supply commercials have made her
a household name. But Sergei wants Polly to
be adorable just for him . . . and Polly isn't one
to follow doctor's orders!

**Watch for DOCTOR, DARLING.
Coming in January 1991**

TDDR

Coming soon
to an easy chair near you.

FIRST CLASS is Harlequin's armchair travel plan for the incurably romantic. You'll visit a different dreamy destination every month from January through December without ever packing a bag. No jet lag, no expensive air fares and *no* lost luggage. Just First Class Harlequin Romance reading, featuring exotic settings from Tasmania to Thailand, from Egypt to Australia, and more.

FIRST CLASS romantic excursions guaranteed! Start your world tour in January. Look for the special **FIRST CLASS** destination on selected Harlequin Romance titles—there's a new one every month.

 Harlequin Books

JT-R

Harlequin Regency Romance™

COMING NEXT MONTH

#41 LUCY'S SCOUNDREL by Barbara Neil
Lucy Bledsoe had suffered a broken heart and
humiliation at the hands of one scoundrel. So when
the opportunity presented itself to teach yet another
ladies' man a well-deserved lesson, she agreed with
alacrity. She had not counted on Lord Roderick's
array of charms or her own fatal attraction when it
came to scoundrels.

#42 THE MARRIAGE BROKERS by Irene Northan
In return for a favour, Miranda Branscombe finds
herself on the auction block for a husband. Guided by
her brother and their childhood friend, Miranda
engages the interest of two very different but eligible
partis, but the courting does not go according to plan.
The marriage brokers must then step in with an
alternate solution, if only Miranda will agree.